"*Leading Team Alpha* narrows the gap between leadership theory and the practical everyday applications of leadership thought in the corporate world. The characters of DandaData are easy to relate to and really bring the everyday challenges of becoming an effective leader to life. A must read for new managers and leaders in all walks of life and professions."

—*Lissa Pohl, MA,*
Center for Leadership Development University of Kentucky
and Certified Lights On Leadership™ Coach

"*Leading Team Alpha* is an intriguing novel that illustrates the skills necessary to lead in the global workplace. Joel creatively interweaves educational theory with practical applications to show what's needed to deal with the complexities of leading in the business world. He articulates the principles of leadership well and shows how great leaders deal with the varying characters and challenges every day."

—*Ashley Brown,*
VP Financial Planning & Analysis

ALSO BY JOEL DIGIROLAMO

Yoga in No Time at All

leading team
alpha

JOEL DIGIROLAMO

leading team
alpha

LEADERSHIP IN
NOVEL FORM

JOEL DIGIROLAMO

PranaPower, LLC
Lexington, Kentucky USA

Published by PranaPower, LLC, 543 Laketower Dr., Suite 118, Lexington, KY 40502
Printed in the United States of America

Woodrow Wilson quotation courtesy of the Woodrow Wilson Presidential Library, Staunton, Virginia.

Cover design, book layout, and illustrations by Trish Noe, Noe Design, Inc., Lexington, KY USA

If you would like to purchase large quantities or a custom version of this book for your organization please contact the author directly.

Library of Congress Control Number: 2010907477

Publisher's Cataloging-in-Publication data

DiGirolamo, Joel.
    Leading team alpha : leadership in novel form / Joel DiGirolamo.
    p. cm.
    Includes bibliographical references and index.
    ISBN-13: 978-0-9770884-3-0 (hardcover)
    ISBN-13: 978-0-9770884-2-3 (kindle)
    ISBN-13: 978-0-9770884-1-6 (e-book)

1. Leadership—Fiction. 2. Success in business—Fiction. 3. Business—Fiction.
4. Executives—Fiction. 5. Software industry—Fiction. 6. Industrial management—
Fiction. I. Title.

PS3604.I387 L43 2010
813.54—dc22   2010907477

*To my father, Joseph DiGirolamo, who demonstrated
charismatic leadership for me at an early age.*

LEADERSHIP

More than 100 years of research, an incredible number of intelligent people toiling, and we still don't have a comprehensive definition of it. But—we know it when we see it.

CONTENTS

ILLUSTRATIONS

FOREWORD BY ROBERT HOGAN

As practical guides to action, most popular books on leadership are, at best, misleading. They are often thinly disguised, self-serving and score-settling reminiscences written by failed former managers and military officers. Many times the lessons offered in these books endorse exactly the behaviors and attitudes that caused the manager to fail in the first place—but there is no way for the unwary reader to know this.

The leadership literature is plagued by two big problems. On the one hand, everyone thinks he or she is an expert on leadership—there are no barriers to entering the business of being a leadership guru—and becoming a leadership guru can be quite profitable. As a result, the leadership literature is one of the largest and most incoherent in the social and managerial sciences—we might call this the tyranny of the amateurs.

The second problem concerns the fact that the professionals—academic researchers—can't agree on any big issues. The academic study of leadership has largely failed. One searches the literature in vain for practical suggestions regarding how actually to do leadership. This reflects the fact that most academics have had very little experience with real leadership challenges. And it reflects the fact that they have defined leadership incorrectly. Most academic studies of leadership define it in terms of the people who are in charge. Think for a moment about the kinds of people who ascend to the top of large, hierarchical, male-dominated institutions. Those people are politicians who, for the most part, have never demonstrated any talent for leadership.

Now comes Joel DiGirolamo's new book, *Leading Team Alpha*, a book with three important characteristics to recommend it. First, Mr. DiGirolamo has abundant and significant practical business experience on which to draw, and this is evident in the contents of the book—sharply observed incidents from real life in "the office." Second, the book is framed in terms of a novel, based on the notion that stories are more accessible and educational than tables of statistics. The book is clearly and briskly written and fun to read.

But most importantly, the leadership lessons that it teaches are consistent with the best modern thinking on leadership. Specifically, leadership is not about having a successful individual career—think, for example, of the long list of highly compensated CEOs who in recent decades have ruined or crippled their companies. Rather, leadership is about building and maintaining a high performing team, a point that emerges forcefully from the study of human origins.

Leading Team Alpha is an enjoyable and entertaining introduction to the best modern thinking on leadership, and virtually anyone interested in the topic can read it for profit and pleasure.

Robert Hogan, Ph. D.

FOREWORD BY TOM WELDON

My relationship with Joel goes back to the earliest days of my business career—Junior Achievement. I still remember calling him to join the "company" I was leading at the time. We were faltering, and I felt that his skills would be a great asset in turning the group around. I was right—he made a tremendous difference in making that company a success. And so when he asked if I would be interested in writing a foreword to his leadership book, I agreed without hesitation because I knew that he understood how business works and what leadership is about.

Leading Team Alpha is a rare book, one that is both entertaining and informative. Think of it as a management primer in a fictional business story. In this tale Joel does an excellent job outlining management and leadership theory and illustrating how it can be applied to everyday situations, leading to superior team performance.

Managers frequently apply the mantra "ready, fire, aim." Although there is much to be said for taking prompt action, there is more to be said for thinking first. *Leading Team Alpha* gives the reader an opportunity to witness the power of thoughtful action.

As you become immersed in the story, you will enjoy following the thoughts and actions of the protagonist as he deals with a dire business situation, seeks outside guidance, builds the trust and support of his team, and artfully maintains a true sense of urgency. The results he achieves are the kind that not only deserve praise and promotion, they are the kind that would make any CEO proud. I hope you find *Leading Team Alpha* as enjoyable and enlightening as I did.

Tom Weldon

CHAIRMAN AND PARTNER, ACCUITIVE MEDICAL VENTURES
FOUNDER AND FORMER CEO AND CHAIRMAN, NOVOSTE CORPORATION

PREFACE

When writing my first book, *All Paths Lead to Now*, I noticed a consistent theme in the feedback—"I really liked the story about..." This caused me to think about stories as teaching aids. As I pondered this teaching modality, it occurred to me how often we remember new material and relate it to others by describing a story we have heard, seen, or read.

And so when I considered writing a book on leadership I felt that I must do so in the setting of a novel.

I am grateful to have had a business career of over 30 years that took me to almost 20 countries for technical, strategic, financial, managerial, marketing, or business development work. I grew up in the soybean fields of Indiana. My father was CEO and Chairman of a public electronics company, and I have visited with hundreds of companies around the world. I have a technical degree, an MBA, and a master's in Psychology. These experiences and educational opportunities have equipped me with the tools necessary to talk to virtually anyone in any type of organization and quickly develop a rapport.

Almost everyone has an opinion on leadership—which is part of the problem. Everyone has an opinion. Mounds of research data and many concepts have been generated in the academic community and yet little has leaked out into the business community. Robert Hogan has an apt description for this duality: the Troubadour Tradition and the Academic Tradition. With mixed success, Industrial and Organizational (I/O) Psychology practitioners have labored for years to bridge this chasm.

One aspect of the problem is that the two communities speak different languages. For example, an I/O psychologist will talk of an "assessment" whereas business professionals tend to call them "tests." In the world of psychology we speak of "cognitive ability," but the concept is better known in lay terms as "intelligence."

Beyond the orientation aspect of the divide lies the difficulty of structure. The business leadership realm is relatively amorphous while the academic leadership tradition has a clear history, evolution, and set of facets, or lenses through which to view leadership.

Leadership research titans such as Bernard Bass, Jim Collins, David Day, Ed Fleishman, John Hemphill, Robert Hogan, Kurt Lewin, Rensis Likert, Fred Luthans, Ralph Stogdill, Gary Yukl, and Stephen Zaccaro have assembled a vast depth and breadth of knowledge for us to draw upon. The only problem is that it rarely gets translated or repackaged for the business community.

Leading Team Alpha is my contribution to bridging this divide. My desire is to bring the leadership research to the business community in such a manner that it is understandable, entertaining, thought-provoking, and immediately useful.

Joel DiGirolamo
joel@jdigirolamo.com
Lexington, Kentucky, USA
2010

ACKNOWLEDGEMENTS

First and certainly foremost, I want to thank my father for showing me what leadership, rapport, and challenge are all about. I have vivid childhood memories of him engaging with everyone he met in the plant he managed. He knew everyone's name, about their kids, their vegetable gardens—and they knew him. I watched as he showed people that he cared about them and challenged them to do their best. He pulled people together to work toward a solution to a problem or concern. I observed my father negotiate with skill, tact, knowledge, and respect. He showed me how to confront a person with honor, speaking with the voice of reason and without ego. He genuinely cared about all of the people he met.

I thank my editor, Beth Connors-Manke, for her patience with me, guidance, attention to detail, and insightful analysis of this story.

And speaking of patience, I appreciate the encouragement, faith, and patience of my wonderful wife, Karen. Through the days, weeks, and months of work, she stood by me and did not waver. Despite my moments of doubt, she said, "You'll get it done, and it will be great." Thank you, my love.

Lastly, I thank all of the people in every corner of the globe whom I have met in this lifetime. They have provided even more lessons, fodder for this story, and companionship through this life's journey.

chapter one

You are not here merely to make a living.
You are here in order to enable the world to live
more amply, with greater vision, with a finer
spirit of hope and achievement. You are here to
enrich the world, and you impoverish yourself if
you forget the errand. —WOODROW WILSON

Dean fidgeted in his chair, awaiting his turn to speak. As he squinted to see the audience behind the bright lights, his thoughts turned inward, to the perils he had avoided to reach this place of honor. It was easy for him to go back to the place where it all began, when he struggled to keep his small, yet powerful team alive amidst CEO demands and corporate intrigue.

Although it was almost two years ago, he remembers that morning's call well: "Dean, did you see what BenSoft just announced? They're saying they're going to deliver your NU technology in July." His gum still popping, Tony continued, "We're toast, pal, unless you deliver soon. Hate to see what this is gonna do to the stock price. Just wanted to make sure you knew. Remember you heard it here first. Ciao, pal."

"Uh, thanks," was all that Dean could muster before the phone clicked on the other end. He despised Tony, his finely tailored Italian clothes, his air of confidence. Antonio Androni, *Italian aristocrat.* It made him want to puke. He always had to be out front, ahead of everyone else. Setting his ego aside for a moment, Dean checked a few news sites and confirmed the announcement. The stock was already taking a hit—down four points to $74 and change.

Dean had feared this day. He knew that NU technology was the future to pursue but had always been held back by minimal funding. While he was lucky to have four very talented programmers, they were only enough to create prototype interfaces and network communication modules. *Things are certainly going to be changing quickly,* Dean thought. *I better chat with Randy.*

Unable to focus on anything other than putting one foot in front of the other, Dean strode down the hall to Randy's window office, relieved to find him there even though he was engaged in a phone conversation. Randy motioned for Dean to enter then returned to his phone conversation. Sitting in one of the guest chairs gave Dean more time to collect his thoughts. *This is not going to be pretty. On one hand the pressure will be on to produce a new version of software with NU technology; on the other this is an incredibly challenging assignment. I hope they don't feel they need someone with more "experience." I've heard that one too many times.*

Glancing at all the awards and diplomas on Randy's wall was intimidating. The master's degree in computer science from MIT seemed to be his crowning achievement. Knowing that most CS graduate students at MIT get Ph.D.s, he often wondered if Randy had bailed out of the program before completion. He certainly wasn't going to ask.

While he had been reasonably successful in his career, Dean often felt inferior with his midwestern computer science degree. Reluctant to go to school out of state, he hadn't even bothered applying to the top tier schools. *Maybe that was a mistake.* He was happy with his move to Ann Arbor, however. The local university provided enough culture and diversion as well as continuing education. It was a nice place to raise his family.

Dean enjoyed managing his small team. He'd spent several months hand-picking the programmers he wanted for the job. They were a close-knit team, enjoying the challenging assignment working with leading edge technology. His role was comfortable, keeping the team focused on gaining experience with the technology and ensuring DandaData was poised to integrate the technology whenever the senior management of the company felt it necessary.

Still surveying Randy's wall, Dean's eyes reached the corporate vision. He'd seen it hundreds of times, but he read it once again. "Viewed as a leader in database software by our customers. Passion for our products and the ways in which our customers use them. Ethical in all our business dealings. Socially responsible."

Randy was a reasonable manager, but Dean would often become irritated when he shrank from the task of requesting more funding for Dean's team. He could sense Randy was winding his conversation down.

Placing the handset down, Randy swiveled his barrel-chested body around to face Dean. "So what's up? You're not looking your usual chipper self."

"Randy, we've got a problem. Have you seen the BenSoft announcement?"

"No I haven't. What did they announce?"

"A new version of their database product with NU technology. Availability is slated for July—only three months from now. The stock has already taken a small hit and I'm worried. You and I both know this could really impact our business."

"Yeah, you're right. What are the details? Are they revving the whole database product, or is it just some communication module?"

"The best I can tell is that they're revving the whole database product, interfaces and middleware. Of course with these big changes there will be early problems, but meanwhile they can cause the market to stagnate and stop all sales. Given NU technology's ability to simplify installation and management, you and I both know that all database software will eventually switch to it. I guess we should have listened to our sales team when they said customers were saying that our competitors were going to be doing something to improve installation and management. So where do you think we go from here?"

Randy began spinning his pen over his knuckles. "Well, we knew it would eventually come to this. Let's just hope it doesn't crater us too badly. Go ahead and gather whatever information you can find. Engage the competitive analysis folks, if they're not already engaged. They're usually pretty quick about finding out about these kinds of announcements. Maybe they can get some inside scoop from a 'friendly' customer. I'm sure Jim's going to want a review as soon as possible, maybe late today or in the morning. Don't worry about the usual CEO review outline, just give him all that you can gather. Eventually he's going to want to know how we can build up your team and match this, but clearly we can't have that analysis for this meeting. I'll see when we can get on his calendar. Can you give me an update later this afternoon?" Randy turned back to his computer to check his calendar. His right arm flung outward, a nervous tick that Dean had seen only once before, when they went through a round of layoffs three years ago.

"How about 4:00 o'clock? Do you think you can have anything then?" Randy asked.

"I'll bring what I've got and see who else should join us. I'll get a room if the group gets too large for your office."

"Thanks. We'll get this figured out."

Dean rushed toward the glass-walled building, glancing at his watch one more time, *7:28, good, I'm not going to be late. Ugh, these early morning meetings are killers.* Placing his badge against the reader, Dean saw the security light turn green. He pulled the heavy glass door open. Still hazy from lack of sleep, he hardly noticed the plush carpet and modern artwork of the DandaData lobby as he advanced toward the second badged door. *Damn badge readers are always slowing me down.*

Making a turn down the bright corridor toward the CEO enclave, Dean enjoyed the pristine white walls and industrial linoleum flooring. Nothing to distract his focus at this early hour. Rounding the final corner to the CEO's conference room, he closed his eyes and wished this were a dream. Tony and Randy were milling outside the conference room in the dark wood paneled reception area. The subdued lighting, deep carpet, wood trim, and artwork always seemed to bring a sense of hushed whispers. A sign might just as well have been placed on the wall saying, "Quiet." While he knew that Tony would be at the meeting, seeing him in real life made him want to pivot on his heel and walk back out.

Tony's athletic form was leaning forward, approaching Dean like a man on the hunt. "Gotta love these 7:30 meetings, eh, pal?" Tony said as he chomped on his gum.

"Yeah, sure," Dean replied, not wanting to engage the conversation.

Tony was fully attired for an audience with Jim—neatly pressed and starched cream colored button down shirt with business blue pleated pants. Dean wondered if Jim cared how anyone dressed, but then reminded himself once again that Tony was one level higher than him: Tony was at the Director level. *Maybe I should upgrade my wardrobe.*

Thankfully, Randy cut in between Tony and Dean. "Did you get much sleep?"

"Yeah, about three hours worth. I sure hope we've got enough stuff to satisfy him," Dean said.

"Don't worry, it'll be fine." Randy's right arm began to flinch again. "Listen, I'll kick the meeting off and then hand it over to you. You OK pitching the whole thing?"

"No problem. It certainly makes sense for me to."

"I noticed the stock closed down eight points yesterday. This isn't looking good."

"I know. Hopefully we can ramp up our development efforts quickly enough that it won't impact sales. Our maintenance contracts should be good for—"

Jim wheeled around the corner as if on his morning jog. He spoke without breaking stride. "Morning gentlemen. Go ahead and have a seat. I need to set this stuff down in my office."

"Good morning sir." Straining his neck toward Jim, Tony piped up before anyone else could get a word in. They filed into the conference room and as Dean began setting up his computer for the presentation he already felt the perspiration running down his armpits.

Tony once again began to speak, intending to have a conversation in full swing when Jim returned. "Randy, I had my team engaged with a few of Dean's folks yesterday to get started looking at the architecture changes we'll need to incorporate NU technology into the existing database product. It's a good thing we both work under you so that our teams can work closely without anyone worrying about turf battles. I think Dean's guys have done a good job showing the feasibility of the concept. We should be able to take what he's got and run with it."

Dean could hardly believe his ears. Tony was already attempting to take charge of the project. *That SOB. He's going to lobby to keep me in the background.*

Jim launched into the conference room, a single pad of paper in his hand, his closely cropped hair still wet after having gone through his daily exercise routine. Clad in a simple polo shirt emblazoned with the logo of a local prestigious golf course, Jim's short stature belied the absolute power he wielded and his impressive pilot skills. Jim owned one of the few privately held MiG-29 fighter planes, capable of Mach 2.4 and remarkable maneuvering capability. He would occasionally use the plane, literally a cockpit perched on two massive jet engines, to attend meetings in Silicon Valley for the day, returning late in the evening.

I wonder if this will be a "good Jim" day or a "bad Jim" day. Given the circumstances, this is probably going to be unpleasant.

"Good morning again gentlemen, looks like we've got a major problem on our hands. What can you tell me about this BenSoft announcement?" Jim snapped. "I'm sure you've all seen that the stock price closed down eight points yesterday. We've got to figure out how we're going to respond. What've you got for me?"

Tony wriggled in his seat, preparing to speak when Randy piped up. "Sir, we've looked at all the material BenSoft has provided publicly and our Market Intelligence group has dug up some more detailed white papers from a consultant. I think you remember Dean Edmonds here, our Development Manager for New Technology. His team has been working on NU technology with a small team of four people in the back room, so to speak, for the last year or so. Of course you know Tony, manager of the current software product.

Just then a tall man with dark hair combed up and back popped his head into the doorway. "Excusez-moi, would it be acceptable if I join you?" he queried in his thick French accent.

"Sure Jacques," Jim uttered as he looked down and waved him in. "I think all of you know Jacques Foucault, our VP of Sales and Marketing. Go on, go on."

"They've built prototype interfaces and communications modules," Randy continued. "Also, our folks who attend standards meetings have heard several people in the industry talking about NU technology. Given the advantages NU technology offers in terms of ease of installation and maintenance, we have no doubt that our entire industry will eventually switch over to it. The question is just how quickly the products will adopt it. Dean will take you through what we know."

"And so, you can see that their announcement is pretty comprehensive. My guess is that they've already got two or three pilot sites up and running," Dean said, winding down his presentation. "As Randy said at the outset, we just don't know how quickly customers will want the technology. Given the long time periods some of our customers use our products, we may be OK. On the other hand, as you saw, with the annual maintenance cost savings with NU technology some customers may be willing to switch fairly soon. Of course, entirely new customers will find it very compelling."

In a rare event, Jim was silent, looking up in thought. No one dared break the silence, not even Tony. Jim turned back to the group with a sober face. "This is about what I expected and it's troubling. Here's what we need to do. Jacques your sales guys need to have their ears to the ground, they need to find out if any of our customers are looking at this. Of course you don't want to go asking them about it directly, but we need all the eyes and ears on it. Randy, when can you give me an estimate on how soon we could roll out a new database version with NU technology?" His mood becoming agitated, Jim barked, "I need to know timelines, resources, funding, the usual."

Randy looked at Tony and then Dean, "What do you think guys, one week? Next Wednesday?"

"Oh, I think we can do it quicker than that." Tony blurted out. "Dean, think we could come back late Monday?"

His anxiety building, Jim shot out, "Listen, I want the answer 7:30 a.m. Monday morning! We're behind on this and one way or another I'm going to get a team to build what we need. I don't care who you need or where you have to go to get it. We've got to get this in gear. Our future is at stake, guys. I built this company from nothing and I'm not about to watch it wither away. Another thing, Jacques, you need to get with the finance guys and look at the potential impact this could have to our bottom line over the next year and a half if these guys here can't deliver. I want some scenarios built with high impact, low impact, etc. Look at what we might need to do for pricing on our product in the short run. Any questions?"

Barely leaving time for anyone to inhale, Jim said, "Good. Let's go. Move! See you Monday."

Before anyone could arise Jim was gone like an owl on its silent flight.

Jacques raised his eyebrows and was the first to speak. "Well gentlemen, it appears that we all have our marching orders. Good luck on your project, and we'll let you know if we hear anything." He arose from the chair, his frame towering over Dean as he leaned forward and strode out.

Not wanting to let Tony muscle in first, Dean began, "Tony, we need to get our teams together this morning and get this kicked off. Randy, do you want to say anything to our teams about how important this is to the business to set the tone? I want these guys to realize what a huge threat this is to our business. There's no question that BenSoft has gone for the jugular."

"I'm right behind you, Dean," stoked Tony. "My guys have a status meeting at 9:00. How about we get everyone together at 10:00? We'll wrestle this baby down to the ground."

"I'll get us a room. Randy, you in? You're sitting there awfully quiet. What's up?"

"I'm just sitting here thinking about all the pieces we need. I'll ask Becky to sit in as well since this will impact her integration team. You guys remember the ancient Chinese curse, 'May you live in interesting times?' I think we've been cursed."

Packing up, Dean wasn't sure what to think. *I'm not sure how we're going to get all of this done by Monday. We've got to figure out all of the code modules we need, how big they might be. Then we've got test, build, integration, alpha and beta tests. How do we split the work between Tony's team and mine? Ugh. How am I going to fend him off this time? The last time we were in a situation like this he ended up cutting me off at the knees by going behind my back to Randy. I hope we don't have to go through that again.*

"Cheer up pals, we'll work it through and it'll be a smash hit. Just you wait and see. See you at 10:00, gents," Tony said as he resumed popping his gum.

"Hey Randy, you still OK to meet now?" Tony queried, hands against the door frame, leaning into Randy's office.

"Sure, come on in," Randy replied, pressing his arms against the chair to lift his body out. Tony glanced around, angling for the proper seat. He reached for the door and gently closed it.

"Sit in the sofa," Randy said as he took a place in a guest chair, his wide frame filling the entire seat. "How was lunch?"

Tony brushed the wrinkles from his neatly pressed slacks. "Fine. A few of us went to the new Indian restaurant on Mayfair Road. Too bad you couldn't join us."

"Yeah, I would have liked to but I need to have this budget update finished by the end of today. So what brings you here?"

"First, I want to thank you for kicking off the meeting on Wednesday. I think it set the tone for the teams on the NU technology project. By the way, we're calling it project Phoenix since this project will need to pull us out of our current disaster. We had another round of meetings yesterday, and I wanted to catch you before the weekend so that you could be thinking about this. I've been thinking about how we separate out the work between my team and Dean's. I'm wondering if it doesn't make sense to just bring his four people into my team so that we can have a tight integration of the NU technology into our existing product. Dean could remain the lead for the team. I'm not sure what other organization would make sense. After all, my team has been working on this code for many years. They know it well. You don't need to give me an answer now, I just wanted to plant a seed to let you think about it."

"Tony, I have given it some thought, but first we need to see how Jim is going to react to our sizings and see how much additional funding we get. I don't know if he'll go for the ten million additional dollars you guys are projecting. I appreciate you sharing your thoughts with me, but let's see what happens on Monday morning."

Looking down at his Italian loafers, Tony replied, "Sounds fair enough, but I don't want us to waffle on this issue too long. I want our teams fully engaged on the project as quickly as possible."

Randy looked down at his watch. "Sure. Well, I really need to get back to this budget. Is there anything else?"

"No, that's it. You going to the game tonight?"

"Yeah, let's hope they pull through this time."

Tony rose slowly, releasing the stiffness in his lanky body. "I really do appreciate your support on this. Thanks."

Dean was the first to arrive. Glancing into Jim's office through the window, he could see Jim aggressively engaged in a phone conversation. *This is not going to be fun.*

Randy strolled up, heavy briefcase in hand. "Good morning

Dean. How was your short weekend? Sorry for the Saturday meeting, but you know how important this is to the company,"

"It's OK. I think we're ready. I reviewed the three development options again, and I still think it's the best we can muster."

"Yeah, really, all other options are just variations of those," Randy agreed.

Jim burst through his door, a serious look on his face, "Where is everyone? We're starting at 7:30!"

"I'm sure they'll be here in a few minutes, sir." Randy looked at his watch. "It's just now 7:30. Did you have anybody else coming?"

"I don't need anyone else. Go in and have a seat. I'll be right there," he said as he turned to go back into his office.

Dean and Randy quietly filed into Jim's conference room just as Tony and Becky were arriving. Randy began to attach his computer to the projector for the presentation. "Good morning guys."

"Good morning...I think," Becky mustered. She remained uncomfortable, once again feeling as if she were in the background while others held jobs in the spotlight. Becky wanted to move up in the organization but felt she was held back by the low perception brought from her third tier school degree. She felt as if no one took her seriously. Despite her strong on-the-job performance, she knew few respected her degree from a less well-known university. In the pecking order, Becky knew it was important to have good academic degrees hanging on the wall. Every time she looked at Randy's collage of diplomas, her confidence took a small hit. She wondered if Tony or Dean ever felt this way.

Dean eyed Becky's smart attire, a fitted skirt with a low cut, lavender blouse that accentuated her athletic figure. He enjoyed how the color brought out the blue in her eyes and highlighted her smooth, straight brown hair. The lack of chatter suddenly came to his attention. *Hmm, Tony certainly seems subdued this morning.*

"Morning, chaps," Tony said as he lifted his coffee mug.

Dean summoned the will to speak to Tony. "So what do you have in your cup today?"

"Oh, just a bit of cappuccino from the old country. Of course, I'll never find coffee here like that back home in Italy, but I certainly dream of—"

Jim swept in, almost silent on his feet, without so much as a pen in his hand. He thrust the door closed with a thud and stood in front of the group. "I'm sure you all have been watching the stock price."

Everyone began to shift in their chairs, assured that this was not going to be pleasant.

"We closed at around $65 on Friday. I just got off the phone with Walter, head of sales in EMEA, and he said they've heard from two of our large customers over there that they're piloting the new BenSoft release. We're starting to get questions from other customers about if or when we'll have NU technology. I want all of you to understand how important your development is to the viability of this company." His eyes shifted to scan everyone in the room, "Is that clear? OK, what have you got?" he said as he took a seat near the screen.

Randy broke the silence. "Sir, I've had my entire team looking at the project ever since we met last Wednesday. I've asked Rebecca Green, Manager of Integration Services to join us. As you recall, all three of these folks work for me, so we should be able to do most of the development in my shop. We're calling the project Phoenix, by the way."

"OK, OK," Jim responded impatiently.

"What I have to show you this morning is three scenarios

we've laid out. As I mentioned, we worked the rest of last week and Saturday on this. Our first scenario is for a 15-month delivery schedule, the second one an 18-month delivery, and the third a 24-month delivery with no incremental funding."

Randy noticed that Jim was uneasy but continued on, bringing up his first slide.

It was almost as if Jim's blood was boiling, his body physically shaking. "Listen, I don't need to see any more of this. I don't care what that last scenario says. Here's the story. We can't afford any incremental funding. If anything, we need to be looking at ways to cut costs. If we start losing sales or customers put purchases on hold, we're going to be hurting, boys and girls. What you guys need to do is figure out how to give me a new release in 15 months without any—without *any* incremental funding. Is that clear? And I want full functionality, not some lame half-assed release. Got it? Come back in two weeks and show me where you are. You can have my AA put it on my calendar. I gotta run."

Blasting out of his seat, Jim didn't look back. Randy, Tony, Dean, and Becky looked at each other, not knowing what to say.

As usual, Tony was the first to speak. "I'd say we've got our work cut out for us."

"Yeah, I guess so. Let's reconvene in my office," Randy uttered. "I've got a bad feeling about this."

Randy flipped through the project estimates again, his right arm moving almost incessantly. "I think we all know what we need to do. We've got to figure out how to do all of the project work in 15 months with the manpower we currently have on board."

Not wanting Tony to gain the upper hand, Dean spilled out, "I hate to bring this up but one card we haven't played yet is utilizing the Bengaluru support teams. I think there are around 50 developers that we could redeploy. This is a big enough deal that I think we could get some of them."

Without hesitation Tony added, "You know, that's a fantastic idea, Dean. Some of those guys have already worked on my code. Given the pay differential, it might work."

"If I extend out the delivery times for my integration projects, I could probably offer up a few folks. I know that every little bit helps," Becky proposed.

Randy was heartened at the spirit of cooperation, a rare occurrence. "It shouldn't be too hard to figure out if that will work. I'll chat with Anil in Bengaluru. Let's see, it's 10:10 our time, so that would be 8:40 their time in India. I'll give him a call on his cell phone and see if I can catch him. Dean, can you run the estimates again to see how many Bengaluru folks we'd need to add?"

"Sure thing."

"Becky, how many do you think you could give up? Two?"

"Yeah, I could do that," she said, flashing her blue eyes at Dean and Tony. "You guys owe me for this, you know."

"Baby doll, you name it," Tony shot back.

Randy glared, "Tony..."

"OK, OK, I get the message. Sorry Becky."

Randy sighed, his broad chest seeming to collapse. "Let me check my calendar. Dean, could you give me an update at 3:00?"

Dean nodded and Randy carried on, "Becky, see who you could shake free in the next couple of weeks, and they need to be top tier, all right?"

"No problem."

Randy closed out the meeting, once again spinning his pen over his fingers. "I'm getting a better feeling about this. Maybe Jim will let one of us fly his MiG to Bengaluru for a meeting."

"Ah, wouldn't that be something. I'd rather get my all my stock options above water, though," Tony blurted.

Randy glared at Tony once again as Dean shook his head. *I didn't get any stinking options. I just wish this guy would shut his mouth.*

Filing into the auditorium, the energy was palpable. Each person was to have been given his or her role in the new organization. Dean watched as each of Randy's employees sat, pushing their spring-loaded, deeply cushioned seats downward, often slumping into a relaxed position.

When the new headquarters building was designed, Jim insisted on an auditorium which could perform double duty—large corporate meetings as well as evening concerts or theatrical performances. Designed into the building with a set of security doors behind and beside it, public functions could easily be accommodated while maintaining security for the rest of the complex.

Randy approached the podium. Tony, Dean, and Becky were seated on the stage to his right. "Please take a seat folks, I'd like to get started." Pausing, his right arm flinching, Randy began. "Thanks for coming out for this exciting announcement. You should all have been informed of some of the changes, although we've kept the overall structural review for this meeting. As everyone knows, one of our major competitors, BenSoft, has announced a new release of their database software which will utilize NU technology."

"Just to make sure we're all on the same page, I want to talk about NU technology a bit. NU stands for Network Ubiquity and is a loose term for a set of network protocols that allow software to be deployed with little human intervention across enterprise networks. This technology will greatly reduce installation time and complexity as well as reducing run-time expense and maintenance. For a bit of trivia, it is also the Internet TLD, or country code top-level domain name for the small island country of Niue in the South Pacific. And no, people assigned to the project will not be relocating to Niue."

Everyone laughed.

"You may have seen it on some domain names, .nu in Sweden, Denmark, or Holland, where it means "now." It also happens to be similar to "nouveau," the French word for new, and of course our English word N-E-W, new.

"Anyway, back to our industry. BenSoft announced their release on April 17th, with availability in July. We've since found out that they have several pilot projects running and some of our large customers are looking at it quite seriously. Of course our stock has taken a hit with this as well. Just before the announcement we peaked at around $78, and now we're at around $64. This is clearly troubling.

"We've had several meetings with Jim Sousa, and where we've come out is targeting the next release of our database product with NU technology in 15 months. We know this is aggressive, but we feel that given your talent and ability we can do it. This is an "all hands on deck" moment, folks. We're going to be asking a lot from you in the coming months because this is an aggressive goal and clearly is crucial to the vitality of our corporation.

"Obviously we'll need to change some roles, and so today I'm announcing a few changes to the structure in my organization." Flipping to the next slide, Randy continued. "As you can see, Tony, Dean, and Becky will still report to me, but their teams will be changing somewhat. Tony Androni will continue as Director of Current Products, Dean Edmonds as Manager of New Technology, and Becky Green as Manager of Integration Services.

"The communications and interface teams that were in Tony's area will be moving to Dean's group to work more closely with the folks who have been researching this technology for the last year or so."

Tony shifted in his chair, uncomfortable with this turn of events.

"In order to bring additional manpower to the project, we've negotiated with the support team in Bengaluru to bring many of them into Tony's area. We realize that there will be a learning curve for this team, but we feel it's necessary to complete the project on time. Finally, a few folks from Becky's team will be joining the New Technology group, although we don't know who those folks will be at this moment. And now I'll turn it over to Tony to take you through his group."

As Dean listened to Tony, his mind began to wander. How would he organize his group? What did he need to do differently with a larger group? *I think I've done a good job with my small group of four, but what will I need for a group of 60? Can I really do this? Where do I start?* Then it occurred to him, a vivid memory from a college course in general psychology. The instructor, Dr. Solomon König, had been an inspiration. His passion for the topic of leadership and genuine interest in applying results from scientific psychological studies to organizations was contagious. While Dean had been reluctant to engage Dr. König in a lecture hall of 150 students, he had enjoyed the few personal conversations he'd had with him. *Perhaps Dr. König could help me with this.*

"Department of I/O Psychology, may I help you?"

"Yes, my name is Dean Edmonds, and I'm trying to reach Dr. König. I'm a former student of his. Is he available?"

"I think he's in a class at the moment. Let me check...Yes, he has a class but should be back shortly. Would you like to leave a message in his voicemail?"

"Uh, sure. Thanks."

"Just a minute, please."

Hearing Dr. König's voice again brought a smile to his face. His vibrant energy seemed to travel through the phone line, bringing a sense of Dr. König's physical presence. *How does he do that? What is that?* The beep on the other end brought Dean back to consciousness. "Uh, Dr. König, this is Dean Edmonds. You were my instructor for Psych 101 seventeen years ago, way back in 1984. You probably don't remember me, but I'd like to chat with you for maybe an hour or so to discuss some leadership issues. I remember your passion for that topic, and I think maybe you can help me if you can spare the time. You can reach me at 743-528-8299. Thanks a lot, and I look forward to hearing from you."

As he hung up the phone, Dean wondered if he'd ever get a return call. He remembered Dr. König talking about the research and business articles he'd written along with his consulting experiences. It seemed that he could rattle off one tale after another. *Am I worthy of a return call in his eyes? I guess I'm about to find out.*

With the cool morning air hanging in the trees, Dean approached the psychology building, a generic red brick college building similar to most in the Midwest. The spring air and familiar footpaths took him back in time to his student days there at the University of Michigan. He could still feel the weight of his backpack, an ever-present weighty companion. Beyond computer science, his psychology and Eastern philosophy courses had the most impact on him. The discussions on human behavior, enlightenment, and gurus remained present in the back of his brain.

Pounding his way up to the third floor, a wave of discomfort came over Dean's body. While the stark white concrete block walls and linoleum floor seemed familiar and comfortable, their austerity clashed with the lush corporate environment he had become accustomed to at DandaData.

Reaching the upper floor, Dean paused for a moment, thrust his hand into his pocket and pulled out his cell phone. *I certainly don't want to be bothered during this meeting.* In an automatic motion, he set the phone to vibrate mode and slipped it back into his pocket.

The hallway wound around the central core. He passed classrooms, the library, and finally arrived at his destination. A simple black nameplate adorned the wooden office door: DR. SOLOMON KÖNIG, PROFESSOR OF PSYCHOLOGY. He squared his body with the door, feeling as if he were about to pass over the threshold into another world. Raising his arm, he lightly tapped on the wooden door frame, causing the frosted glass window to rattle.

A muted, "Come in," was heard in response. Dean turned the

doorknob and slowly entered the office as the professor swiveled in his chair to face Dean. While Dr. König had certainly aged since he last saw him, his rugged face and full salt and pepper beard looked very much as Dean recalled. His unmistakable thick, wiry hair was still evident as was his athletic body. Dean wanted to smile, noticing he still wore his trademark flannel shirts over his broad frame.

"You must be Dean."

"Yes I am, Dr. König—"

"Sol, please. I don't need any of that doctor nonsense. Glad you could make it. You're fortunate I had this opening. I was to be in California on a consulting assignment, but these business people can sometimes be quite fickle, canceling at the last minute. So you say you were in my Psych 101 class many years ago. I'm flattered that you remembered me."

"Oh, I couldn't forget you! Your class, along with Eastern Religions, was far and away one of my favorites here. I enjoyed your enthusiasm and the passion you had for bringing the science of psychology into organizations. Your energy was contagious."

"I see. Have a seat. Well, I guess I did a bit of good teaching you undergraduates, then. I always wondered if anybody was awake in those classes. Being semi-retired, I currently teach only a graduate level seminar, and I don't have to worry about it much now."

Glancing around the room Dean noticed the starkness of the concrete-walled office was softened slightly by the overloaded wooden bookshelves lining both side walls. Scanning the titles, they seemed foreign, yet familiar. *Power in Organizations, Real Managers, The Nature of Managerial Work, Management and the Worker.*

"So who did you say you're working for again?"

"A software company. We make database products that enterprises all over the world use in their back office systems," as he reached into his jacket pocket. "It's a pretty big company. We're about six billion dollars in annual revenue. Here you go," Dean said as he handed Sol his business card.

"Dan-du-data. Funny name for a—"

"No, it's pronounced DON-du-data. Danda is Sanskrit for staff. The name is meant to imply that we help businesses create a stable foundation."

"I see. Enough of that. What brings you here and how can I help you?" Sol straightened himself and folded his hands on his lap.

"As I mentioned, I have a computer science degree from the University of Michigan and have managed a small software team for about the last year and now will be growing it to about 60 people in the next several months. So, I think I need to hone up on my leadership skills. I've read a few business books on leadership, but they all say different things and are clearly just someone's opinion. I'm confused.

"I remember you talking about leadership research and was thinking that maybe you could give me some more concrete advice, something with a bit more meat on it."

Smiling and raising his hands in the air, Sol responded, "Dean, the leadership research over the last century is a funny animal. The truth is, we've studied it extensively, and we still can't tell you what it is! It's truly like the blind men on the elephant—different people have a view of different aspects. I've been in this field for almost 50 years now and frankly *I* can't give you a definitive answer."

At this Dean wondered if he should just thank Sol for his

time and slink out the door. An uncomfortable silence filled the space.

"In fact, some people will say that leadership really doesn't matter. But we know that's not true. Look at John F. Kennedy and his goal of putting a man on the moon by the end of the 1960s. Look at Lee Iacocca and his dramatic turnaround of the Chrysler Corporation from 1979 to 1981. Part of the problem is that we've not been able to get a good measure of leadership... OK...are we done? Should we talk about something else now?" Again Sol folded his hands in his lap.

Becoming more uncomfortable, Dean wasn't sure what to make of this cantankerous professor. *Am I just wasting my time here? How do I get out of this gracefully? Why is he pushing me away?*

"I'm sorry, Dean. Sometimes I get on my soapbox and let it fly. Do you want a bit of the history first?"

"Sure, the background would definitely help, wouldn't it?"

"Absolutely. Let's take it from the top so to speak..." Belying his 78 years of life, Sol popped up out of his chair and grabbed a marker at the whiteboard. He began a diagram...

"Back in 1849 a man named Thomas Carlyle wrote a book called *On Heroes, Hero-Worship, and the Heroic in History*. In this book Carlyle put forth what is usually referred to as "The Great Man Theory," that great men are born, not made. Much as psychologists have argued over whether intelligence and behavior is caused by nature, genetics that is, or nurture, that is our environment, they have argued over whether leadership is born in an individual or created by the leader's environment

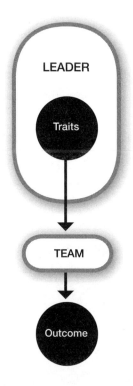

FIGURE 1. *Trait leadership model*

and can be taught. So this is what I like to refer to as a constructive model. In other words, a Great Man is constructed of many parts. It's sort of like the archetype models. A Great Man would be one specific archetype. And notice that this is the Great *Man* Theory. At the time it was thought that women could not be leaders, of course.

"Then psychologists went on a kick of what was called "trait-based leadership" research for decades. They were looking at what people *have*. They looked at everything from height, weight, speech, energy, to intelligence, extraversion, and on and on. This is what I refer to as a deconstructive model because now we are looking at the individual parts that might make up a good leader. One good leader might have a certain combination of parts and another leader a different combination. So now let me ask you, how many traits do you think they found were desirable in a leader?"

Dean squirmed in his chair, buying time for a response. "Oh, I don't know, maybe 30?"

"Only 30?" Sol quipped, smiling, "Is that your final answer?"

"Should it be higher?"

A broad grin came across Sol's face. "OK, enough of this game. I've seen lists with as many as almost *200* traits! Is that useful?"

Dean thought for a moment, then replied, "How in the world would you keep track of that many? I can't see how that would be helpful."

"Exactly! So, in 1927 an Industrial and Organizational Psychologist named Walter Van Dyke Bingham wrote a paper stating that leaders weren't just born that way, but could learn and grow from a nascent potential to a wise, experienced leader. This led to a stream of research into the behaviors of leaders. At the time it was felt that a leader's behaviors were a result of their traits."

"Then in 1939 a group of social psychologists named Lewin, Lippitt, and White set up several group dynamics experiments. They arranged and observed three types of groups: authoritarian, democratic, and laissez-faire. The results showed that the group situation has much to do with how the groups work and their outcomes. This led to a shift in leadership research to a situational approach."

"Two now-famous leadership research programs began in the 1940s—one right here at the University of Michigan and the other at Ohio State University. These programs opened up new

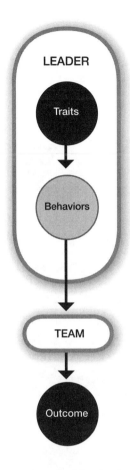

FIGURE 2. *Behavioral leadership model*

avenues of research on how leaders adapt to individual situations.

"Ultimately this led to a focus on how leadership is as much about the *person* as it is about the *process* of leadership. Let's complete our model so we have the whole picture.

"So once again, here we have our leader. A leader is born with some traits, which we think of largely as intelligence and personality. These traits, among other things, cause a leader to

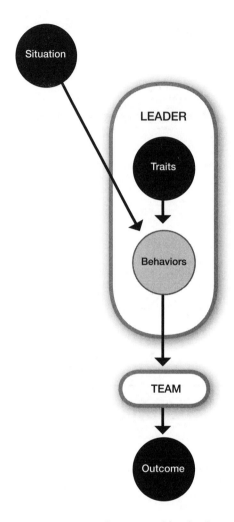

FIGURE 3. *Situational leadership model*

behave a certain way. The behaviors are what a team sees, and of course the team produces some outcome. So what do you think of that?"

"It makes sense, but why do you show the situation outside of the leader?" Dean replied.

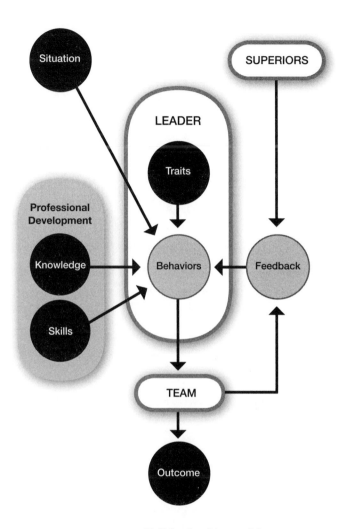

FIGURE 4. *Full leadership model*

"Ah, because the situation also acts on the leader to influence the display of specific behaviors. Can you give me an example?"

Thinking for a moment, Dean replied, "OK, how about this? I have one team member whose performance could be better. I meet with him more frequently so that I can help him along, to keep him on task and provide assistance when he needs it. Another person is a very high performer. She's self-disciplined, has a strong work ethic, and is very creative. I basically leave her alone and just check in occasionally to make sure she's headed down the right path and to get an update on her status. So for me, I lead each person in a different manner, depending on their situation. Is that what you mean?"

His bright eyes widened and Sol responded, "Yes, exactly. You've got it! So let me ask you this, can you change your traits?"

"Well, no, I don't think so."

"Correct. It's not likely, although it does happen in some individuals when they have a profound experience in their lives. So in general you can't change your traits, but as you've described, you can change your behaviors. Now my next question is, what other factors might change your behaviors?"

Smiling, Dean replied, "Hmm, if my boss comes in and 'suggests' that I do something differently, I either have to argue with a good reason not to do it, or comply with the suggestion."

Laughing, they both understood the situation deeply. Dean felt his cell phone vibrating and chose to ignore it, immersed in the conversation.

Sol continued, "Yep, the boss and that paycheck can be a powerful influence! So, leaders adapt to superior feedback, but also to team feedback. This can change a leader's behavior if they are open to change—but more about that later. So we still have two more factors that can change a leader's behavior, knowledge and skills. What can you tell me about them?"

"I guess I can think of one. When I go to a conference or sometimes a meeting with other software managers, I learn something that will give me an idea of how I can work differently with my group. That would be changing my behavior, right?"

"Yes, so that's knowledge. The other is somewhat related—skills. When you learn new knowledge and skills you also change your behavior—hopefully for the better! This is why good leader training is important."

Dean stretched in his chair and nodded his head, smiling. "I still remember a quote from Lord Acton that I heard in a philosophy class: 'Power tends to corrupt, and absolute power corrupts absolutely. Great men are almost always bad men, even when they exercise influence and not authority...'"

"Oh, you mean like Jeff Skilling of Enron or Bernard Ebbers of WorldCom?" was Sol's rhetorical question. "Yes, unfortunately it's true, and frankly I've found that there are a lot of bad leaders out there—ones who could be helped with some training and guidance. The corruption is another thing, and there are sound psychological reasons for how they become corrupt. As leaders achieve more through assertive actions and possibly innovative methods they begin to feel entitled to many things. But enough of this. We must move on or we'll be here all day.

"What we've learned over the last 100 years is that we can take these somewhat fixed traits and complement them with knowledge and skills that are acquired to grow leaders into meaningful, very powerful and productive roles. What must be kept in mind is that what works in one situation will not always transfer to another situation, and that a leader who works well in a given role may not work as well in another. And further, what is required to be a leader at a lower level in an organization is very different than what is required at the top of the organization.

"Dean, let me pose this to you, when I ask you to name charismatic leaders, who comes to mind?"

"Let's see. There's John F. Kennedy, who you already mentioned and Martin Luther King, Jr. It seems to me that they had a significant effect in shaping the world over the latter half of the 20th century."

"OK, good, good. Now, what is it about those two individuals that makes you say they are charismatic?"

Dean looked up in thought and responded, "I guess there is something about them that draws me toward them, makes me want to follow them. I have faith in them and, well, it seems that they have an interest in me and our society collectively. Is that what you're looking for?"

"Yes, good. We know from research that charismatic leaders have a sense of mission which they eloquently communicate and which we can easily buy into. We have faith in these leaders and want to be associated with them. Of course there is a dark side to charisma. Take Adolf Hitler for example. Great leader. He influenced a tremendous number of people to commit atrocities. In fact, that is how I ended up in America. My family fled persecution under his regime in Germany when I was 14. Charismatic leaders can have a powerful influence and therefore must use their power wisely and ethically. People are often afraid of charismatic leaders because they have seen the damage that they can do.

"And further, charismatic leadership is an element of what we sometimes call transformational leadership. This is a style of leadership that influences followers with inspiration, intellectual stimulation, and individual attention—in addition to the charismatic element. You can contrast that with the alternative, what we Industrial and Organizational, that is, I/O, psychologists call transactional leadership, which may produce results, but not at the level that a transformational leader would."

"Sort of like when people talk about the difference between managers and leaders? Is that what you mean?"

"Yes, it's similar, but these are all shades of grey, Dean."

Having sat for so long, Dean became restless and rose to the whiteboard. "OK, this is all good and pretty theoretical, but I need something concrete, maybe a list of things a leader does." Grabbing a marker, he asked, "Can I write a list?"

A smile came across Sol's face once again as he uttered a loud sigh. "Oh Dean, you business people are always trying to pin us down to a list or bullet points, or whatever. OK, OK, how about this..."

Having created the list, Dean and Sol sat back in their chairs to look it over again...

- Intelligent
- Knowledgeable about factors affecting the team
- More comfortable amongst a group of people than alone
- Agreeable with others
- Open to new ideas
- Emotionally stable
- Conscientious
- Committed
- Humble and selfless
- Adaptable to different situations, acts appropriate to the situation
- Intervenes poor performance appropriately
- Respects all individuals

- Decisive
- Ethical
- Trustworthy
- Energetic
- Confident, self-assured
- Follows through, dependable & responsible
- Creates a vision, mission, goals
- Plans well
- Aligned with the organization
- Communicates well with team members
- Involved with the team
- Communicates well with superiors
- Communicates well with others, including customers
- Facilitates discussion
- Resolves conflict well
- Listens
- Collaborates
- Develops people
- Utilizes positive reinforcement effectively
- Maintains focus
- Seeks out and utilizes self-development opportunities
- Promotes creative tension, challenges
- Motivates and inspires
- Acquires resources
- Uses resources wisely
- Breaks down roadblocks
- Protects team members
- Empowers, delegates
- Trusts team members
- Develops relationships

- Good interpersonal skills
- Provides guidance and instruction appropriately
- Negotiates well

Sol looked at Dean once again. "And so you see why I'm reluctant to provide people with a list! There are too many items to keep track of. As humans, we have difficulty keeping track of more than seven to nine things at a time. This list is useful as an occasional reminder to a leader, however, and is certainly a good list for evaluation and diagnosis."

Dean's eyes were glazing over. Staring at the list once again, he said, "I'm not sure what to do with this. I definitely want to write them all down, though."

"Dean, leadership is a lot of things. Just remember, anything you do that aids your team in moving forward to achieve its goals is leadership. I'll tell you what, we've been at this a while and frankly I'm tired of sitting. It's a crisp day. How about if we continue this discussion over a walk?"

Dean brightened up. "Sure."

Dean felt the warmth of the sun on his chest and breathed in the invigorating, clear air. Although they were walking slowly, Sol's steps were strong and deliberate. Dean turned the conversation back to leadership. "So Sol, you've been very helpful to me explaining what leadership is about. I've also got to think about who to put into my leadership positions. How can I choose? Is there a way to discover who is a charismatic leader? I don't know any charismatic programmers!"

Sol returned his now-familiar smile. "Well Dean, quite a

few people have spent a lot of time trying to answer that question. It is very difficult. You saw how long that list was on the whiteboard. How do you test for that? I'll tell you this much: we know that intelligence and some specific elements of personality play a large part in being able to predict who will turn into a good leader.

"There are many assessments we use to measure cognitive ability, or intelligence. We also frequently use a personality assessment called the Big Five, or the five-factor model. Have you ever heard of that one?"

"No, I've only heard of the Myers-Briggs test. I'm an ENFP!"

Chuckling, Sol responded, "I see. Well, the Myers-Briggs test certainly is the most common personality assessment, but the problem is that it's not been found to predict leaders well. Let me explain. The Big Five personality characteristics are the following:

- Openness
- Conscientiousness
- Extraversion
- Agreeableness
- Neuroticism

"Think of the acronym OCEAN to remember them. Studies have shown a general trend where some of these elements will predict good leaders. It's a bit more complicated than that, but that's a discussion for another day. You can also do interviews that are very consistent and measurable, called 'structured interviews.' And finally, many organizations use what are called 'assessment centers' to identify individuals with potential leadership skills."

Stopping and turning toward Dean, Sol stroked his beard and began to bring the conversation to a close. "Dean, I recommend you work with your HR department on this. Look at the assessments we've just talked about, but be sure to ask two important questions, what job analysis has been done, and, how the assessment validity is determined. The job analysis is to determine the essential tasks for a given job and the validity will ensure you are measuring the correct attributes. Can you remember that?"

The words were coming to him slowly, but Dean managed to utter, "I think so, but you've hit me with a fire hose here. Is there anything I can read on all of this?"

"There are certainly many sources on how to do this, the problem is that it's not a 'one size fits all' kind of thing. You have to read across several disciplines to understand all of this. I've written a few books on leadership myself, but they're quite specialized and not too useful to you in this moment. How about if I send you some information or at least some sources?"

"That would be great, but I don't want to take any more of your time Sol."

Blinking, he said, "It's my pleasure, Dean." Sol hesitated and stroked his beard once again, a distant look in his eyes, "You know, I shouldn't have pushed back so hard when you first came in, Dean. My purpose in this lifetime is to help people. I hope I've helped you in some way. Now that my teaching load is minimal and I don't do research any more, I certainly have more time to help folks like you. If you need me again, please give me a call. I do want to be available for you."

Dean's eyes lost their focus and he felt Sol's touch on his body. Not a physical touch, but an energetic touch. He was lost for a moment, feeling a connection with Sol in this short time and a head filled with more information than he could comprehend.

"OK, let me digest this and see what I can do with it."

"Sounds like a good idea. I'm sure you'll have questions. Really, don't hesitate to give me a call."

Glancing at his watch, Dean asked, "Sol, you've given me a lot of help, can I at least buy you lunch?"

As he shook his head, Sol smiled and replied, "Not necessary my good man. I bring my own. I'm not going to stay healthy eating cafeteria food."

"I see. Well, if I can ever do anything for you, please let me know."

"We'll stay in touch," as Sol cast a hearty smile.

Dean thrust out his right hand and looked directly into Sol's deep brown eyes, again feeling that close connection, as if they'd known each other for decades. Sol grasped Dean's hand, completing the connection on a physical level.

"Thanks again, Sol," Dean replied. Slowly turning, the surrealism became palpable. It was as if he were in a trance when in Sol's presence. *How does he do that?* Slowly, he felt himself again crossing that imaginary threshold, this time to the outer world. It seemed difficult to believe that two hours had passed. As Dean retraced his steps back to his car, he felt as if the world had changed. He took a quick glimpse back at Sol and was surprised to see him still standing there, smiling, hands in his jacket pockets, a knowing look on his face.

Thoughts swirled in Dean's head. *How do I digest all of this? How does it affect my team? What do I do differently? How am I going to figure out how to select my team leads? Who do I talk to? Talk to... Hmm, I wonder who called?*

Pulling his phone out of his pocket, Dean saw that is was someone from DandaData. *I wonder what that was about...*

chapter two

Spectacular results emerge from great seeds nurtured by elegant processes.

"Message one. Received at ten twenty-six today. Beeeeeeeeep."

"Hey pal, this is Tony. We're looking for you. Two of my team leads and one of your guys are getting together with me for a quick meeting at 10:30. We need to make some decisions on this third party vendor for the plug-in. I'll try your cell phone, too. Ciao. Beep.

"Message two. Received at eleven fifty-three today. Beeeeeeeeep."

"Hey pal, Tony again. We missed you at the meeting. Just want to give you a heads up on our architecture review meeting today. One of my guys, Brad, will be there. He's a good team lead candidate for you, so keep your eyes and ears open, K, pal? Ciao." Beep.

Great, he's probably wanting to dump someone on me. I can't imagine him willing to give up an "A" player. I know that deep down he really doesn't want me to succeed. Thanks, Tony.

"Hey Dean, got a few minutes?" Dean looked up to see Randy in his doorway, his wide frame obscuring Dean's view of the hallway.

His shoulders drooping, Dean replied, "Sure Randy. Want to have a seat?" Dean motioned toward a chair at his office table. *I really don't need this right now...*

As Randy fell into the chair his body seemed heavy and serious. "The first thing I want to check on is how you're coming on filling the team lead positions. You know we need to give Jim an update in a week, and we need to show some progress."

Feeling tightness in his chest, Dean said, "Yeah, I know. I've been working on it. We've already agreed on Anton, right?"

"Yeah."

"Since he and I began the NU technology work, he's got a lot of history and knowledge. He's my key guy. As for the rest, I'm still pulling the list of candidates together."

Randy's face crinkled and he began to respond. Dean's mind wandered to his family. *Surely I could be in a better spot in this moment.* Dean had often wanted to move around, finding better jobs with each move, but his wife Jamie had discouraged this. She had felt, rightly so he thought, that their children would be better served with the consistency of growing up in one town. *Maybe staying here wasn't the right decision after all.* Tuning back in to Randy...

"Tony offered up Brad. He's been a great coder and has shown some creativity with the database engine enhancements in the last two revisions. He might be a good asset to your team."

Ooh, how am I going to dodge this one? Brad did come up with some nice innovations but he neglected one of the major components and caused a three week delay.

Dodging the heart of the issue, Dean replied, "Yes, he has done some good work, but I'm not sure if he fits the profile of a team leader. Do you think he has the people skills?"

"I'm not really sure that's important for the job. What's important is that he knows what's going on technically so he can keep the project moving forward. I've been around a lot of projects in my time, and believe me, it's important."

Choosing to yield for the moment, Dean replied, "Yes, you're certainly correct, but let me think about it for a few days. Is that OK?"

"Yeah, I guess so." Randy's arm began to flinch. "And have you and Tony drafted what we're going to show Jim next Monday?"

"No, I was going to schedule something with him on Wednesday or Thursday."

"Mmm." Randy's voice tightened. "Look, this is serious stuff. You know Jim's not one to mess around. You remember the story about him firing the customer service manager as he was giving his presentation? He didn't like what he was hearing, told him he was incompetent, go back to his office, and clean out his desk. Then he looked right at that guy's manager, pointed to him and said, 'Next time bring in someone who has a brain, got it?' That was the end of that meeting. I don't want to get pointed at like that!"

"Yeah, I understand. I think we've all heard the story a time or two... Look, how about if Tony and I run through our pitch to Jim with you Thursday afternoon so that we have Friday to make changes and get any more information that we might need?"

Sitting back in his chair, Randy relaxed a bit. "Look Dean, I'm worried about this project. It's clearly got a lot of visibility and risk. Not a good combination. I don't want to fail, and I don't want you and Tony to fail. I want all of us to succeed."

Randy looked around Dean's office. "When I was in grad school at MIT I knew it would be hard, I just didn't know how hard... If I had known how hard it really would be I probably wouldn't have started... I know this is a hard job, too. Now what can we do about filling these team lead roles? What's your plan?"

"I plan to finalize the list of candidates in the next couple of days, and I'm hoping to have a decision and announcement by mid-next week. Will that be OK?"

"Yeah, I think that should be good, but we can't go beyond that." After considering the matter a bit more, he continued, "It means we'll go into the meeting with Jim without those positions filled. Is there any way you can get them filled and announced by Friday afternoon? You've got four days..."

Dean's frustration was building. He repositioned himself to sit upright at the table, facing Robyn. "My mind is trying to get a handle on all of this. Looking at my notes, let me see if I can summarize your proposed leader selection process. First, you interview the existing team leaders, their managers, and team members, and they tell you what they feel is important, such as college degrees, skills such as written and verbal communication, tasks they do, and so on, right?"

Robyn nodded, her straight blonde hair and long blue earrings falling forward. "Yes..."

"That's what Dr. König calls 'job analysis,' right?"

"Yes, correct."

"Then you figure out what factors might be most important

and find or create tests, or 'assessments' as you like to call them, that would work for us."

"Yes, you've still got it..."

Looking at his notes again, Dean continued, "And then... you run the existing team leaders through the process and compare their job performance with all of their scores to see what measurements will predict which people will make good team leaders. Do I have it?"

"Yes, that pretty well sums it up." Flipping her hair back to look Dean straight in the eye, she smiled at him and said, "I know it sounds complicated, but it isn't actually that bad."

Dean frowned, shaking his head. "Umm, so the fifty thousand dollar question is, how long is all of this going to take? It sounds like an incredibly long process."

Still looking straight at Dean, Robyn replied, "Oh, I'd guess four to five months before we're ready to assess your first candidates. Why?"

Dean felt as if he'd been hit with a bat. As Robyn had gone through a proposed process, his mind kept saying to him *this is going to take too long, this is going to take too long,* but hearing it was another thing. His voice tight, Dean pressed on. "Robyn, you don't understand, I just don't have that kind of time. I need to get these positions filled by Friday and today is Tuesday. This just isn't going to work. What can we do? You know, this is the kind of stuff that gives you HR folks a bad name. Can you please be more responsive?"

Robyn could practically feel the hair on the back of her neck stand up. *HR unresponsive. Ugh.* After taking a calming breath she sighed and looked down at her papers, unsure how to respond. She could lecture Dean on how important it is to perform the proper job analysis and assessment validation and hold firm to her ground; she could try to find something to help him in the short term; or she could lash out at him, letting him know how totally unrealistic he is and walk away from the project.

Allowing herself to settle into a rational approach and realizing that a middle path is often the best, she rose, straightened her blue and white floral print dress and began, "Dean, I understand your frustration and also realize that you're under the gun here. Let's start with the leadership model you've drawn on the whiteboard behind me. As I said, this is a perfectly fine model. Let me overlay the aspects of selection on it."

Standing at the whiteboard she began to draw and explain, "Let's start within the leader. First, and most importantly, it is well known that intelligence, or General Mental Ability, what we often refer to as GMA, is a primary factor in job performance. Secondly, some aspects of personality are known to contribute to overall job performance. Now, over the long term we would want to look at motivation assessments, creating a structured interview, and possibly some situational judgment assessments.

"Moving over to knowledge, it's pretty easy to find out what your existing team leads have and what is important. Then, again for the long-term, we can look at creating a specific set of skill assessments. Finally, as you can see five elements are left out. In my view, these can be wrapped in as elements of our culture here at DandaData.

"And so as we work on the long term project, all of the cultural elements will automatically get included in the process. As the managers, team leaders, and team members talk about what is important to them for their job, a significant part of what is important is related to our culture. Does that make sense to you?"

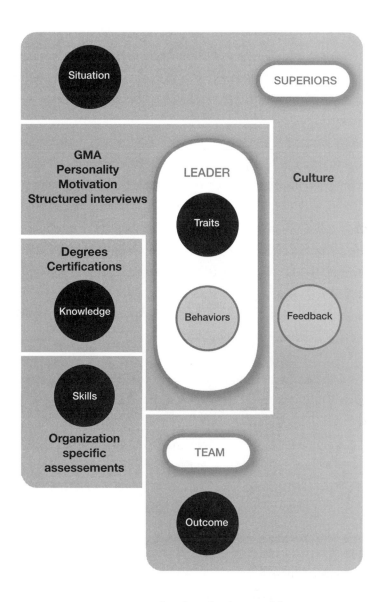

FIGURE 5. *Leader selection model*

"Yeah, I think I see what you're saying... You're saying that we could do an intelligence assessment and personality assessment for this project to help make my short term decisions, and you could also do the in-depth work for us to use at a later date. Is that correct?"

Robyn stood with the whiteboard at her side, looking blankly at the far wall. It was a difficult thing for her to say, feeling as if she were compromising her values. Closing her eyes, she took a deep breath. Slowly opening her eyes, Robyn turned to Dean and gave an affirmative nod. "Yes... that's what I'm saying."

Robyn continued, a bit more freely now that she had given her proposal, "I don't like doing this, but I understand the urgency for the business. We can have the candidates take the assessments online fairly quickly, and you and I can discuss the results. You have five positions to fill, correct?"

"Yes."

"And how many candidates do you have?"

"I've got seven on my list right now, but expect to have another two to three. Is that OK?"

"Sure, that's no problem. Normally we only use this process for our executive slots here, but we've been wanting to move it farther down into the organization. We made a couple of runs at creating a process for first-line managers and team leaders before, but no one in management in the organization was willing to sponsor us on a project, so we gave up and crawled back over here to our HR 'cave.'"

They both chuckled and Robyn continued, "If you and your manager are willing to sponsor us on the project, I think we could go ahead and begin. Right now we've got a lighter load than usual so we could definitely fit it in unless something else comes up. We never know what Jim might throw at us... I think this would make a good project and would be enormously helpful to the organization."

Robyn brightened up. "So it's becoming more clear to me as we speak. Here's the deal: I'll help you with some quick assessments to get you out of your jam this week and next. Then you and your management agree to help us with the job analysis and assessment validation for the team lead roles over the next six months or so. How does that sound for a deal?"

Dean thought for a moment, then replied, "I think I could sell that to Randy... OK, deal."

Robyn looked straight at him with a smile on her face. "Oh, and one more thing, Dean. Don't *ever* say HR is unresponsive, all right?"

Smiling and looking straight back at her, Dean nodded his affirmation. "You got it!"

Early for the meeting, Dean strode into the CEO reception area. With no one else in sight, he assumed he was the first one there. However, sliding past the first doorway to the conference room revealed something more ominous. Jim was in his usual seat near the head of the table, facing the far doorway. Opposite him sat Jacques Foucault, both remarkably engaged in conversation for 7:20 a.m. on a Monday morning. *Must be important. This might not bode well.*

Dean struggled to eavesdrop on the conversation, but only bits were discernible, "...very concerned... large accounts... defecting... desperate... lost in the dust..."

"Hey pal," Tony announced.

Startled, Dean looked back, forcing a smile. "Hey. Good morning."

His coffee mug held out front, Tony gestured toward Dean. "Ready to get our grade today?"

"What?"

"Our grade. You know how Jim sometimes gives us a grade before we leave—and it's rarely an 'A.'"

"Oh, yeah. I don't know. It doesn't seem to matter much as long as he doesn't fire me. I have to say it's not very inspiring, though."

Shifting his weight toward Dean, Tony leaned in, his eyebrows rising. "Listen, if you want to get to Director level, too, you're going to have to learn how to tell your folks what you want. There's a big difference between running a small technology group and a large, mature software development group with many team leaders. You learn to be assertive and direct. I know, I've been doing it for quite a while."

Dean wanted to run. He could practically feel the pressure of the coffee mug against his chest. Hearing muffled voices, he wondered if Randy and Becky were approaching. He hesitated and hoped for an intercession. At the first sight of Randy over Tony's shoulder, he welcomed them. "Good morning Randy. Hi Becky."

"Folks, come in!" Jim commanded from the far doorway.

While Randy moved toward Jacques to connect his computer to the projector, Dean followed in behind and tried to assess Jacques' body language. *His shirt's not too disheveled, maybe this won't be such a bad meeting after all. He doesn't look too beaten down.*

Jim began, even as Randy continued preparing his computer

to project on the screen, "Gentlemen, and lady." He nodded at Becky. She straightened up in her chair and simply smiled back.

"Since we last gathered, Jacques and I have been to visit several of our large customers both here and in Europe. It's not surprising to report that every single customer is asking about NU technology. They want to know when we're going to have it. We all know the sales and technology cycles are quite lengthy; however, every single one of them understands the compelling advantages of NU technology. The sense I'm getting from these folks is that they won't even consider us in their next round of database upgrades if we don't have NU technology. I don't think I need to say anything more about the situation than that. Understanding what our customers are thinking and that they will likely will be acting with their budgets and wallets is enough for us. I can't stress this enough—the NU technology is key to the continued vitality of this company."

His voice rose as he got up out of his chair. Dean began to wonder if he was going to bound across the table. "Let me say it another way. Your delivery of the NU technology release is crucial to your continued employment here. I can envision a scenario where DandaData, without NU technology, becomes absorbed by BenSoft or another software company, a vestige of its former self. Thankfully, Wall Street seems to be holding out hope for us since the stock has stabilized in the low 60s. That's all I'm going to say for now." Sitting back down, his voice became more calm, but Jim spoke through his clenched jaw, "Let's see what you've got for me today."

No one moved; their eyes simply shifted while Randy finished with the computer and projector. Jacques forced a tight smile. *Looks like I was wrong. Maybe I should be somewhere else. There's got to be an easier job at another software company.*

Despite the diatribe, Randy had managed to get the projector working and rose to the front of the room. Standing next to the screen, his glowing agenda on display, he began, "So Jim, as you requested two weeks ago, we're going to take you through the status of project Phoenix. Today we're mainly going to focus on the schedule, staffing, and coding progress."

Jim simply stared at him, impatiently pressing his pen into his pad of paper. Dean and Becky glanced at each other as Tony leaned forward to speak, then reconsidered and leaned back into his chair.

Advancing to the schedule slide, Randy continued, "In order to meet a GA, or general availability date of July 23rd next year, we've scheduled our full function beta testing to begin April 23rd. This will give us about two and a half months of beta testing before our final build. As you can see, we've put multiple checkpoints in place in order to track progress along the way. So far we're looking good on our progress."

"As for staffing," he said while proceeding to the next slide, "You can see the projected ramp-up line and the actual. We also have the breakouts for coders, stress and stability, quality assurance, and at the end our team leads." Nervous that Jim might lash out upon seeing that the team lead staffing was behind schedule, Randy shot a quick glance at Jim, then to Tony and Dean. Seeing no reaction, he felt the need to bring up the point in the most minimal way possible. "Of course, as you can see we aren't concerned about stress and stability and QA resources this early in the project, and we are just a bit behind in identifying all of the team leads for the project. The work is continuing at the pace it needs, so we don't currently see a prob—"

"What? You don't see a problem without your team leaders in place?" Jim exclaimed. "How about the teams under these guys? Are they in place—as they should be at this time?"

"Well, sir," Randy stammered, "We have a lot of the staffing in place, and we don't currently see a schedule problem."

His piercing glare projected at Randy, Jim's jaw tightened. "I can't tell from that graph, exactly how many team leads should you have on board today and how many do you have? What's your status with that?"

Swallowing hard, Randy replied, "Uh, well, sir, between Tony and Dean's team we should have about 12 on board, and we actually have nine."

Tony inhaled and turned toward Jim, preparing to enter the fray. "Sir, I think we'll be OK. We do have all of the team lead positions in my area staffed, and my guys are continually working with Dean's on the new communication modules."

I can't believe he just said that. He really needed to bring up the fact that all of his positions are filled. Easy for him. He already had his team in place because it's existing technology. Thanks Tony. Gee, maybe I can return the favor some day.

Dean felt it was time to defend himself. "Uh, sir, I'd just like to say we view these team lead positions as crucial to the success of the project and therefore we're being quite judicious about who we put in the roles. In fact, we're requiring candidates to take several objective assessments to help us in our selection. Of course, the drawback is that it sometimes takes a bit longer to fill the position."

All eyes were on Jim, who simply stared back at Dean, then turned to glare once again at Randy. His well-developed muscles rigid, the tension in Jim's body filled the air. Continuing to press his pen into his paper, Jim glanced down at his pad. "Continue. What else you got?"

Randy forced himself to continue. "Sir, our last slide just shows the coding modules we've planned for the project and work is progressing on all modules that are scheduled for work at this time. So, our current view is that while the staffing is a concern we don't see it impacting our schedule at this moment. That's all, sir."

Once again all eyes fell on Jim as he looked down, seeming to collect his thoughts. Looking up and fixing his piercing gaze at each person individually for an instant, he said, "Listen to me, I'm glad you folks are making progress. This is good. But—and listen to this carefully—this... project... cannot... fall... behind... schedule." His brow raised, he spit out, "Does everyone understand that?"

"Yes sir," they replied, nodding their heads.

Smiling and once again looking each individual directly in the eye, he responded, "Good, see you in two weeks—with lots of progress!"

chapter three

The desire for safety stands against every great and noble enterprise. —TACITUS

Dean arrived at the conference room early, connecting his computer to the projector once again. *I wonder if Tony will behave himself? He may be upset that I didn't take Brad, but the guy just wasn't qualified for the job. The assessments showed that.*

Imagining the chairs filled with his five new team leaders plus Randy, Becky, and Tony, Dean rehearsed some of the sound bites he planned to use during the announcement. *...the first time we've used objective assessments for positions such as these... more scientific... you've been chosen to deliver...*

Glancing up, he saw Becky. "Oh, hi Becky. How are you this morning?"

"I'm great." She flashed her bright smile, and their eyes met for an instant. She was clutching her notebook against her chest, making Dean wonder what she was protecting. Dean thought she looked like spring, with her relaxed yellow linen pants and top.

Leaning in toward Dean, Becky lowered her head, glanced back at the doorway and continued, "Dean, I don't think Tony was fair to you in the meeting with Jim on Monday. He could have backed you and Randy up instead of grandstanding." Putting her notebook on the table, she continued, "I mean, it was really disgusting. We should all be in this together instead of backstabbing. Everyone should be looking out for one another. After all, look at that vision statement on the wall. There's that statement about being ethical in all of our dealings. He's a borderline as—"

"Hey pals, where is everyone?" Tony barked as he entered, coffee mug leading the charge.

Stunned, Becky swung around, raising her tightened body to its full height, squaring her body with Tony. While certainly not matching Tony's stature, no one would accuse her of acting diminutive. Grasping her notebook once again and pressing it against her shapely figure she forced a response—"Good morning Tony"—and turned for the nearest chair.

Dean, hoping to avoid the entire encounter returned to the computer and projector as other attendees filed into the conference room. After several trials, his org chart finally came to glowing life on the screen. Dean looked up, glanced around, and saw that everyone had arrived.

"Good morning folks. I want to welcome all of you to our little kick-off meeting for Team Alpha. That's what I'm calling our team since it is really about a new beginning and being in the lead."

Tony shifted in his chair, looked down at his coffee mug, then turned to look Dean straight in the eye.

"I'll begin by introducing everyone and then you can each

give a brief introduction. To my right is Randy Philips, then three of our new team leads, Gary, Sarah, and Betsy. Next, this is Tony Androni, on the other side of the table, our other two new team leads, Frank and Anton. Finally, on my left is Becky Green, Manager of Integration Services. I want to make sure that everyone knows a little about each other. Randy, you're right here next to me so why don't you start."

"Sure, thanks, Dean. All of you know me, I'm Randy Philips, VP of Development, the second level manager for all of the software development."

"And so, you can see from this staffing chart that we still have many roles to fill, lots of open spots on the org chart. We're anticipating that some of those individuals will come from Tony's team, Becky has offered some people up, and the rest will come from other areas of our organization. I want to emphasize once again that we've not been given the authority to hire anyone new."

"It goes without saying, this project is vital to our company's future, so we've got to deliver a high quality product on time. Anyone have anything else before we go?"

Tony grasped his coffee mug with both hands and leaned into the table. "Folks, I just want to reiterate that we've all got our work cut out for us. We know this is an aggressive project, one with great urgency, of utmost importance and of course with that double-edged sword: lots of visibility. I've told my team that they must be working closely with you folks if this project is going to succeed and I think they realize that. We're all in this together, and we truly need to act as one team."

Gee, that's not what he was doing on Monday. What's the deal with this guy?

"Let me know if there is anything I can do for you folks or if my guys aren't being responsive." Leaning back, he straightened his heavily starched shirt. "And best of luck to you!"

"Thanks, Tony," Dean responded. "Randy, would you be willing to wrap it up with a few words?"

"Sure. I think that Dean has put it quite succinctly. Project Phoenix is truly crucial to the future of this company. Please keep this in mind as you work through your staffing decisions, task identification, and goals in the next few weeks. I look forward to working with each of you new folks more closely, and for those of you moving over to Dean's group from another group, we're happy to have you here. Thanks again."

"That's all that I have for everyone. For you team leads, if you could hang around for a few more minutes that would be good. Becky, Tony, Randy, thanks for joining us."

"I'd like to cover a few administrative things before we disperse. First off, I have a staff meeting every Monday morning at 9:00 a.m. I like to review the previous week's progress, discuss any dependencies, work through difficulties together, and talk about what everyone has projected for the week ahead."

"We've got to focus on getting staffed up in the coming weeks and I'll be talking to each of you separately about that. Remember, don't talk to anyone individually about coming to work for you. Always go through their manager first so that you don't cause a problem for the current manager. Now, one last thing. We know what the end goal is for the entire project but I believe it's important for each one of you to have goals for your team. Be thinking about what those goals might be over the next several days and then I'll be meeting with each of you individually to review them. Any questions?"

Dean looked around and saw eyes returning his glance or looking down, nodding in agreement. "Boy, you're a quiet bunch. I hope you don't stay that way! Let's go do it, then. Thanks!"

His computer and notepad under his arms, Dean exited the conference room, his mind racing with thoughts of all the tasks and activities he needed to get done. *How in the world are we going to staff up the remaining 50 positions? Where are we going to get these folks from? I know Tony will fight me tooth and nail before giving anyone up, at least anyone worth having. And how am I going to pick? How do we set the goals? Are they really that important? Maybe I should visit with Sol again. Perhaps he can help...*

Hesitating once again in front of that frosted glass and oak door frame, Dean reflected back to that feeling of entering another world, Sol's world. A place where time stopped and something energetic took over. It seemed magical. Dean raised his hand, hearing the glass rattle once again as he rapped on the wooden frame.

"Come in," was the now-familiar muffled response.

As he turned the knob and swung the door open, Dean recoiled at the powerful scent of salad dressing intermingled with another strong, yet undecipherable odor.

"Welcome, my good man!" was Sol's cheerful voice, swiveling in his chair to face Dean. Somehow it seemed incongruous to Dean to see a man smack in the middle of Michigan in a plaid flannel shirt eating salad with chopsticks. *Sol's an individualist, that's for sure.*

"I'm sorry, I didn't mean to interrupt your lunch. Do you want me to come back in a bit?"

"No, no, not at all. I'm just finishing. Besides, I told you to come at one o'clock, and 1:00 it is. Have a seat. I apologize for the smell. So what brings you back?"

"Sol, I first want to tell you that I very much appreciate your advice on choosing my team leads. So, I'm thinking that maybe you can help me understand how to choose people to go on the teams."

"I see. It sounds like you've had an exciting week and a half! You've also gotten a lot done in that short amount of time. I commend you for your progress. First I want to make sure that I remember correctly. These are development teams, is that accurate?

"Yes, they're writing software for a new version of our database. Why do you ask?"

"Because there are different types of teams with different characteristics. They have differing needs. For example, an executive team would have characteristics quite different from a production team, such as yours, or a customer service team. Am I correct in assuming that your teams will need to innovate and produce a release of code in a given time period?"

"Yes, that's it exactly. And you bring up a good point. One of the thoughts I've had is how to bring about a creative environment for my teams."

Sol perked up. "Ah, I love these questions! Let me see what I can pull out." Spinning his chair back around, Sol opened his lower left desk drawer and began rifling through the well-worn folders, each distinguishable from the others only by the name written on the tab. Dean pondered what knowledge they held. *I wonder if they're class notes, consulting notes, or what.*

"Here we go. I think this will help." Pulling a folder out, Sol leafed through the first several pages, springing upright as he came to the object of his search. "Yes, let's take a look at this," he said, turning the page toward Dean.

Creative Teams
- Right, diverse mix of knowledge & skills brought into the team
- Effective team processes
- Safe environment to share views
- Value conflict & resolve it appropriately
- Time to gain experience and working knowledge
- Individual & team self-development
- Empowering
- Forgiving of mistakes
- Inspiring, knowledgeable leadership
- Appropriate resources

"I put these together several years ago for a consulting engagement. The first item is what you originally asked about, how to choose team members. Research has shown that, similar to leaders, good team members have strong cognitive skills—that is, they're intelligent. We've also found similar indicators through personality research. The one interesting twist is the creative part. Remember we talked about the five-factor model last time?"

"Yes, and that's what our HR person, Robyn, also suggested."

"Good. Did she talk about the role of conscientiousness?"

"Not specifically, why?"

"As I mentioned last time, conscientiousness is one of the factors in the five-factor model, and the one most often used to assist in the prediction of job performance."

Sol's eyes lit up as he continued, "A fascinating research study was recently done to see if personality played a role in creativity. Sure enough, they found that creative and adaptable individuals are more open to experience. That's not too surprising, but they did find something else interesting. They discovered that those who were highly adaptable, that is had an ability to perform well when tasks are changing, scored low on some of the facets of conscientiousness. So the intriguing part is that if you want creative workers their personality might be less conducive to getting the job done!"

A broad smile on his face, Sol stroked his beard and aimed his twinkling, yet piercing eyes directly into Dean's. "And so my friend, the dilemma continues."

Breaking Sol's gaze, Dean blinked, then looked upward, thinking as he spoke, "So what you're saying is that the conscientious people may not be the creative ones?"

Sol continued looking at Dean. The professor's smile remained, but his eyes betrayed a chasm between them. *Is he thinking or traveling to a distant place or memory?* Dean wondered.

"Balance, Dean. Balance," Sol said, the distant expression remaining. "Think about it for a moment. I'm sure you've seen very conscientious workers; those who keep their heads down and crank the work out. Right?"

Dean nodded. "Yes, I've seen workers like that."

Gradually Sol came back into the present. "Good. And you've probably also seen very creative people who aren't grounded. They create one thing after another, but nothing seems to come of their creations. Seen any people like that?"

Dean simply nodded his head as Sol continued on. "But what

you want are those individuals who are both creative and highly productive, correct?"

"Yes..."

"So that's the difficult part, finding the creative, productive individuals."

At this point Dean felt lost again. "I just don't understand, Sol. It seems very difficult. I would think that there are very few of these people and that it's hard to find them and figure out who they are."

Sol smiled at Dean and nodded his head. "Yes, you're correct, Dean. It is difficult to find folks like this, but they are out there. At the minimum, I hope that I've brought the concept of creative and conscientious workers into your awareness. You can then take these concepts and once again work with your HR people if you want to pursue this perspective. Do you mind if I mention one more thing about this diversity element?"

Dean laughed. "Sure, but once again you're throwing a lot of material my way!"

Barely hesitating, Sol plunged on, "It is vitally important to include a mix of individuals on your team. When you have a homogenous team in terms of knowledge, skills, and abilities you might as well not have a team. Everyone will be thinking alike. Teams bring value to an organization when individuals from different disciplines and backgrounds contribute their knowledge and experience to a new problem. If the environment is considered safe for each individual, then they will eagerly contribute and create something great. Does that make sense to you?"

"Sure, of course. But really, I first need to know who to bring onto the team," Dean replied.

Sol stroked his beard. "Hmm, sorry, I got excited and jumped the gun there. But, what did your HR person say about selecting your leaders?"

"She said that she'd need to find some tests to give to people who are leaders already and compare their performance with their test scores to find out what tests correlate with performance. The ones that do she'd use to help us to decide who to pick as leaders."

"I see. Let me ask you this, then. How is selecting your leaders any different from selecting team members?"

"Now that you mention it, I guess it's not really any different. So I just need to follow that same lengthy process?"

Smiling, Sol responded, "The true answer is yes, but you can probably do something quite quickly. You could probably use that assessment for conscientiousness and openness that I mentioned as well as a structured interview, one with very defined questions and some measurement for the responses. You'll need to work with your HR person on it, though."

"I guess I can go back to her. I'm still on her good side for the moment!"

Flashing a knowing smile, Sol replied, "Yep, you don't want to get on the wrong side of your HR folks. They can truly be quite valuable to you.

"One more thing, Dean, and then we probably should wrap it up for today. You must quickly put some goals into place. You'll need specific, challenging goals. We have a considerable amount of research showing that reasonable but difficult goals will improve performance. You're already in a bit of a predicament since your end date is fixed, and so you'll need to create individual contributor goals that align with your overall team and project goals. It is also imperative that you gain commitment from each team member for those goals. You and your team leaders can work with each individual to create the goals, but don't stress over that too much. Research has shown that as long as a team member thinks the goal is reasonable they will likely commit to it. Does this make sense? Does it help?"

The thoughts in Dean's head were already churning. *Sure, I could break the big goals down into little goals for each person. We could break down areas of work and individual code modules. And then there's the testing... I think I could do this...* As he raised his head and saw Sol staring at him, he wondered how long he'd been out of contact. "I'm sorry Sol. You just got me to thinking about how I could break down the Team Alpha goals."

"Huh?"

"The Team Alpha goals—oh, I'm sorry, we call the group Team Alpha because we want to view ourselves as the top dog, so to speak.

"I see. Well, anyway, if this is causing you to think, then I guess I've done my job!" the professor said as a broad smile came across his face. Sol hesitated, then asked, "Any more questions, Dean?"

"No, I don't think so."

"OK, then." Sol popped out of his chair and extended his strong arm. "Good luck Dean. You're certainly on the right track. Let me know when you need more help."

As Dean stood and looked at Sol he once again felt that piercing gaze reaching deep within his soul. *How does he do that? I hope he can't see too deep!* "Thank you once again, Sol. Your help is really invaluable."

"It's what I'm here for, Dean. Keep in touch."

As Dean turned toward the door and saw the hallway, that other-worldly sensation washed over his body once again. *This is like a wave of energy. What is it about this place?* Shooting a quick glance backward to see if anything was amiss, Dean then composed himself and crossed that threshold back into the bustling workaday world.

"I think we're all here, so let's get started," Dean began. "First off, I want to thank all of you team leads for being here this morning. As I mentioned in the meeting invitation, this is an important meeting for us. Based on the inputs we're getting from the other managers and team leaders, I think we'll have no problem filling the slots we've got open.

"All of you have described the knowledge and skills required for your jobs and for the most part, narrowed your candidates down to a manageable group. We know a fair amount about most of the individuals, and we're now down to our final selection. This has been a tough task since we have so many qualified individuals. As I've told to each of you separately, we've had each candidate take a personality assessment to help us make a final decision.

"Let's keep in mind that we're trying to build Team Alpha into a high performance team. I want us hitting on all cylinders, cranking out an awesome product. We've got a lot of inventing to do in a short amount of time, and it's got to be a reliable, robust product. You all know that we have a challenging assignment.

"Some of you have met Robyn Harkle from our Human Resources department. I've asked her to join us today to take us through the results of these assessments, to help us understand the basics. While she can help us with the interpretation of the results, she would like for us to have a general understanding of the process. So Robyn, I'll let you take it from here."

"Thank you Dean. By the way, you did an excellent job describing our process. I think you're beginning to get the hang of this by now. Gee, maybe we can recruit you into HR some day."

Everyone chuckled as Dean smiled and shook his head from side to side.

Robyn continued, "Before we get into the main part of the meeting I want to mention the importance of diversity on your teams. It is very important that you have individuals with different backgrounds so that all of you are not thinking alike. For example, I would imagine that it's good to have someone who has user interface experience on your team as well as someone who has a deep background in computer communications. Together these two people can create a very functional and feature-rich product that should be very easy for your customers to use. Does that make sense to you guys?"

"Oh yeah, I can relate to that," Sarah chimed in. "At a company I used to work at, we were building an audio editing program. We had a bunch of highly technical guys working on it, and they kept coming up with fancy features to change the levels, fades, equalization controls and lot of other effects. The problem was that the novice users looked at it and had no idea where to start. Needless to say, the product bombed in the market."

"Yes, good example, Sarah. Thanks for sharing that. All right, on to the task we have at hand. One of the assessments that your candidates have taken is called the five-factor model, also known as the NEO PI-R. This model measures five facets of personality: openness to experience, conscientiousness, extraversion, agreeableness, and neuroticism. Think of the acronym OCEAN. Probably the most important element is conscientiousness. Numerous studies have shown that job performance is correlated with conscientiousness. If you think about it, it makes sense that your good workers will be conscientious about completing their tasks.

"As Dean just mentioned, for Team Alpha creativity is an important concern. He and I have talked about this before, but we want to take you folks through it. A recent study found that individuals who could adapt well to changing tasks generally were higher and lower in some of the factors than in others. Of course this adaptability is related to creativity.

"What this study found was that adaptability was correlated with feelings, or insightfulness and spontaneity, actions, or being imaginative and adventurous, and ideas, or having wide interests and being idealistic."

"So, you mean that my daydreaming is really useful?" Anton blurted.

More chuckles arose.

"Hey Anton, I don't think that's going to make it into your job description," Sarah added.

"I got it, let's have 'imagination amalgamation' sessions!" Gary shot back.

"I see you guys are definitely into the spirit of this concept," Robyn said as she tried to reel the conversation back in. "There's more, though. As I said, conscientiousness plays a part as well. It was found that those who were lower in some of the conscientiousness elements were, in general, more adaptable."

"Great, so you mean that I should bring on guys who aren't organized or thorough? That doesn't make any sense," Gary asked.

All eyes were on Robyn. "That's not exactly what I'm saying. It's never as black and white as that. Here, let me give you an example. You guys are all programmers and will have programmers on your team, right?"

Everyone nodded. "Yes, that's correct," Dean replied.

"All right, then. How many of you can say that you know of

at least one coder who pretty much takes the input of the team leader or project manager, goes back to their cubicle and cranks out the code?"

"Yeah, I know those folks," Anton replied as everyone else agreed.

"Would you describe these coders as conscientious?"

"Yeah, I'd say so."

"Good. Would you classify them as creative?"

"Well... not always," Gary responded.

"Right!" Robyn exclaimed.

Raising his hand, Dean added, "I think I can give a good example... About a year ago Anton and I were reading about NU technology and began talking and meeting to discuss how we could incorporate it into our products to improve installation and usability. As a result, we both had some current work at that time that slid out because we were not spending our full time on it. So, in your model we weren't as conscientious as we could have been, right?"

"That's right Dean. Good example. So what we're talking about is looking at some of these elements to make a final selection. At this point, all of the candidates would probably be very good ones for you, but let's give this a try to help with a final selection. To keep bias or prejudice out of this, I'm going to be showing you the scores with just a number to identify the person who took the assessment. I've also taken the liberty of putting each candidate into one of three buckets: definitely pick, maybe pick, and lower tier. As I mentioned before, none of these folks are bad candidates, so I didn't want to label the bottom group, 'don't pick,' or something similar. So, here are the results..."

"Listen, I don't understand what the big deal is. We know what the goal is: get the next release out in 15 months. We've got our end date, the full function date, and the pilot date," Tony argued. "Why do you think we need all these interim checkpoints and milestones? I already told you, Dean, you just need to direct your team and stay on them."

Dean paused to relax. "Listen Tony, I think it's really important. It gives our programmers some goals they can reach in the shorter term. This will help motivate them. Do you want to get to the full function date and find out we're not going to make it?"

"OK, OK. What do you think we need again?" Tony shot back.

"I'd like to break the project down with several milestones. Especially if we're going to use the team in India. Can we work backward from the July date and see how much time we have for each individual component?"

Becky admired how Dean remained calm while navigating through Tony's disagreeable behavior. Feeling compelled to back Dean, she spoke up, "Tony, that's what we do for our integration projects. They're mostly short projects, but if they're not we break them down so that they are. I've had a lot of experience with the folks in India, and they really need the structure."

"Alright, so let's work back from our final release date, to pilot test, etc." Tony conceded. "I'll tell you what, Dean. Since you want this so much, you get your guys to come up with a proposal, and I'll take that to my folks and we'll put it together. Sound fair?"

"Yeah," Dean replied as he let out a sigh of relief. "Thanks, Tony, I appreciate you working with me on this."

Dean turned to Becky, sensing she had something to add.

"Well guys, I don't think you need me in here anymore. So, I'll just be moving on..." Rising, she added, "Oh, and remember, keep all the weapons on the table. I don't want to hear about any 'accidents.'"

Dean looked up at her and smiled, feeling comfortable that she seemed to understand the situation and was willing to back him. Tony looked down at his neatly pressed pants, brushed away the lint and responded. "Sure, Becky, thanks."

"No problem, we'll get through this. See you guys later."

Waiting for Becky to leave, Tony began once again. "Are you feeling better now, Dean?" Tony poked. "You've got your high level goals. Can we talk about staffing now?"

"Sure," Dean replied, a sense of uneasiness arising.

"I'm just not comfortable separating out the communications and interface guys from the main database engine. I think these folks need to work closely together, and I'm afraid they won't be if they're partly under you and partly under me."

"I understand your concern, but I don't personally share that view. Plus, Randy has already announced the structure, and we can't change it again this quickly." Dean left the silence hanging, leaving it to Tony to speak if he cared to do so.

Tony looked down, admiring his clean, stiff shirt and contemplating his next move. Lowering his voice, "I'm still not comfortable with it. Let's see how it goes." He then looked Dean directly in the eye, leaned toward him and entered his personal space. "But remember, I'm really not happy about this staffing arrangement, got it?"

"Got it," Dean said through clenched teeth.

chapter four

A good final result requires all the ingredients the recipe calls for.

Dean checked the entry doors and saw the traffic beginning to diminish. "Let's go ahead and get started. I see that a few people are still straggling in, but I think we've got most of the folks here. First, I want to welcome all of you on Team Alpha to our first group meeting. We're now close to our final size of about 60 people. Look around you. You will see your teammates, the folks that you will be spending at least one third of your life with for the next year or so.

"As all of you know well, we will be building the communication and interface modules for the DandaData software with NU technology. Our GA date is July 23rd of next year. We all know we have an aggressive schedule, but that's half the fun. The other half is creating reliable, robust software that is easily used by our customers.

"Your challenge is to do that in the next year. We know that things won't always go smoothly. We'll have some setbacks along the way, but we must persevere and work through the difficulties. We must work together. I want all of you to know that I expect each and every one of you to work together, to help each other out.

"I do not give lip service to the word 'teamwork.' All of you will learn over the course of the next year that one of my most frequent questions will be, 'And who have you asked to help you on this problem?' Do not come to me for answers, but I welcome you to come to me for guidance or to make a decision in direction, if necessary. Do not get possessive, do not undermine your teammate. I will tell you now, I have a low tolerance for such behavior.

"So let's look at the challenges we have ahead. We must innovate and create. We must create new software that will work with legacy systems. We must test and modify. We must test some more—and debug. We must run pilot builds with customers, fix, debug, and test even more.

"But in the end, all of you in this room will have achieved something great... You will have created a fantastic product on a relatively short time schedule. And you will have had a good time doing it with a group of people you like.

"Looking back, I expect that you will be happy with your achievements, maybe even wondering how the hell you did it. You will have been a part of an experience of a lifetime.

"And now I'd like each of the team leaders to come up one by one to give an overview of their part of the project and introduce their team."

"Hey Advay, it's Tony Androni here. Good evening!"

"Oh, hey, good morning, Tony. What's up? We've gotten the week off to a good start."

"Great. Look, I just wanted to let you know that Dean will be sending the Project Phoenix schedule to you this afternoon. We've spent a long time working on this schedule and we know it's aggressive, but we're under a lot of pressure here to meet it. Can you take a look at it and let us know what you think?"

"Sure, I can do, Tony."

"Now Advay, I want to emphasize that we're not giving you a padded schedule, that we're working on identical schedules, so it's very important that you hit the milestones, all right?"

"Right. I've got it Tony. We'll definitely take a look at it and get back to you. We will do it."

"Sol, I think I'm starting to get this leadership stuff, but I seem to have trouble pulling all the pieces together. It seems like I work on one piece of the puzzle and then there's a problem with another area. In addition, we've got this continual voice in the background telling us to keep moving and get this project done on time. Can you help me see the big picture?"

Sol thought for a moment, then looked Dean straight in the eye and slowly replied, "Dean, I think it's time we talked about the leadership process. I haven't talked about this yet because I wanted you to digest all that we've talked about before. But perhaps it's time."

A smile drifted across Sol's face and his energy seemed to rise. "So let's get to it, then. Another fun part!" Springing from his

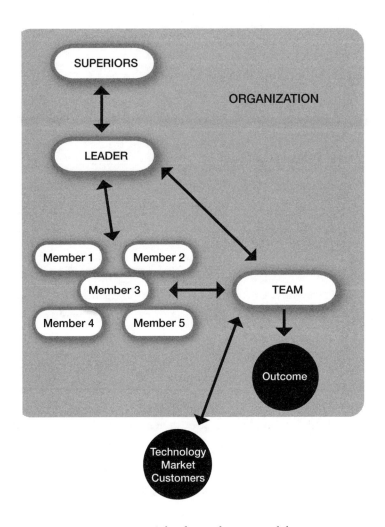

FIGURE 6. *A leader and team model*

chair, Sol began to write on the whiteboard. "Dean, leadership really has five basic functions: creating a vision and continually focusing the group energy and intention on that vision, building a high performance team, motivating team members, ensuring alignment with superiors and the environment and gathering necessary resources, and lastly, maintaining the satisfaction of all members in order to minimize dropouts."

"Hmm, can you explain more?" Dean said.

"Of course, Dean. First let me draw the model and then let's go into each function separately."

"A leader generally reports to one superior, but in reality must work with many different people above. On the flip side, the leader has subordinates who report to him or her who make up the team. Now, the team must have some outcome and is also affected by external forces such as technology, the general market, and customer needs and desires. So now let's look at how leadership fits into this model. Let's start with the relationship of the leader to the team. We talked about charismatic leaders, correct?"

"Yes. We talked about John F. Kennedy, Martin Luther King Jr., and Lee Iacocca."

"Good. As I've mentioned before, one of the most important aspects of leadership is focusing the effort, keeping focused on the vision, on the goal. In an organizational setting it is also good to have a mission. In this case the vision is what you want to be, what you want to become. The mission is what you want to do. A vision statement will consist of many nouns whereas a mission statement will contain many verbs.

"So let me ask you, Dean, do you have a vision statement and a mission for your team? What did you call it again, wasn't it some Greek letter?"

"Alpha, Team Alpha."

"Ah yes! Now I remember, you want to be the big dogs."

Dean smiled but hesitated. "I often remind the team what the goal is and we've got some milestones in place, but we've

Joel DiGirolamo

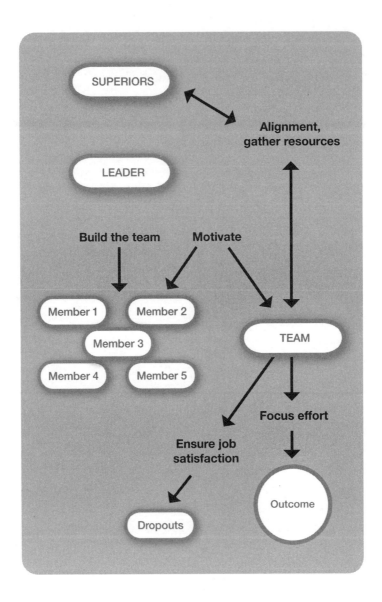

FIGURE 7. *A team leadership process model*

not really worked on a mission statement. I didn't think it was necessary, I mean, we know what we have to do."

"It may not be necessary to have a mission statement in your case, Dean, but it wouldn't hurt. Just don't have five meetings to decide it!"

The joke lightened Dean's mood and he opened further. "I think I can work on that... I think I've got that, what else?"

"All right, so focusing the energy and intention of the group is the first and most important function of being a leader. Now let's talk about building a high performance team. As I mentioned before, decades of personnel research has shown that there are two elements consistently related to job performance—general mental ability and conscientiousness. Remember we talked about that five-factor model a while back? Here it is again.

"You will need individuals on your team who will have a good balance of working toward the desired outcome and keeping a watchful eye on new ideas that might improve your product or service or lower your cost. This is a factor we talked about last time, called openness. Good team members will ask probing questions, challenge your assumptions in a collaborative way, and bring up alternative ideas. Given your history and the work you did with your original team I don't think this is an issue for you. Am I right?"

"Oh yeah, definitely. I've told my folks that it's part of their job to ask the question, 'Is there a better way to do this?' I agree, they should be challenging and asking questions."

"Good. So you've got an idea of what it takes to build a high performing team. I get the sense that you have a close team that works well together."

Dean fidgeted in his chair and smiled. "I like to think so, but

I don't know if that's everyone else's opinion. Maybe I'll find out someday, and maybe it will change if we don't get our project finished on time!"

"True, true. But I'll bet you've found that it's easier to attract people to your team if they have a good overall perception of how you work and what your goals are, no?"

"Oh, I've definitely noticed that. I'll frequently have folks ask if I have openings in my group!"

"Ah, excellent, Dean. Maybe I don't have to teach you so much after all!" Sol quipped. "So let's move on to the third element. Once you've got folks on board you need to understand what motivates them. A lot of leaders think they need to provide incentives or rewards to get people to perform. Considerable research has been carried out on what motivates people, yet controversy remains. The general consensus, Dean, is that individuals are either intrinsically motivated, extrinsically motivated, or amotivated, that is, not motivated at all. The latter are the easy ones. They don't have a place in your organization. You got any of those?"

"No, fortunately I don't, but then I've hand picked all the folks I've got."

"Good, now let me ask you this. What drives you to make Project Phoenix successful?"

"I guess it's about the challenge, about solving a difficult problem, and completing the task."

"Excellent, my good man. So you are a good example of someone who is intrinsically motivated. You have an inner desire to achieve. In general, those are the people you want in your organization. They take less care and feeding. Extrinsic motivation is the desire to achieve so that you will get some reward. Think salesmen here. They are the group most frequently motivated in this manner. Use of extrinsic motivators may be fraught with peril. Some studies have shown that once you introduce an external reward, such as money, you may destroy the intrinsic motivation. In other words, once you use extrinsic motivation you can't go back. Does this make sense?"

"Oh definitely. Now I understand a bit more about the differences between sales people and development folks. In the past I'd always wondered why they were so concerned about their commissions and going to the top achiever sales club the next spring. I just enjoy doing a good job. Interesting..."

"So we've got two more leadership functions to go. Have I worn you out yet?"

"Not quite, but as usual, you're overwhelming me, Sol!"

"Yeah, yeah, I understand... Bear with me a bit more, Dean. So now let's look at the interface a leader has with his or her superiors. From a larger perspective, all groups must operate in harmony with their environment to be successful. This is true on any scale, from a team inside an organization to the actions of all human beings on our planet. In an organization, you must ensure that the vision and goals of the group are congruent with those of the organization as a whole. Further, each group must have the necessary resources to meet their goals. Resources can take many forms: people, money for training materials, software, hardware, etc. Dean, let me plow on through the last topic... Ready to talk about hygiene?"

"Say what?"

"Hygiene."

"Sol, are we going to talk about bathing and teeth brushing?"

"Not quite, but close. Bear with me. We're going to talk about the topic of employee job satisfaction. It's an important one, but often not well-understood. Many people believe that satisfied, happy employees will be productive employees. Unfortunately that's not what research has shown us. The evidence shows that job satisfaction really affects turnover.

"A considerable amount of work was undertaken by a man named Frederick Herzberg in the 1950s and 60s. He determined that many of the workplace elements fall into one of two buckets, either a motivator or a hygiene factor. I think we all know what a motivator is, but what's a 'hygiene' factor? A hygiene factor in Herzberg's world is one which maintains employee health. It's one of those things you have to do, sort of like, as you say, teeth brushing and bathing. These factors act to keep employees in their jobs and are related to job satisfaction.

"Herzberg found that individuals were generally motivated by achievements and being recognized for the achievements. He also discovered that challenging work assignments and growth opportunities were important. Not surprisingly, these elements are consistent with intrinsic motivation. So make sure that you are recognizing individuals and teams as well as identifying growth opportunities for them.

"Now for the hygiene factors. These are elements such as company policies, supervision and relationship to the supervisor, work conditions, status, and security. Think of these as the minimum criteria to keep your employees in their seats. When employees become dissatisfied with some of these elements they generally don't work less, they just leave. So there you have the basics of the leadership process, Dean. Ready for a quiz?" "Oh my gosh, Sol. I don't think so! I've really got to digest this..." Dean sat for a moment while Sol simply looked at Dean with a contented smile.

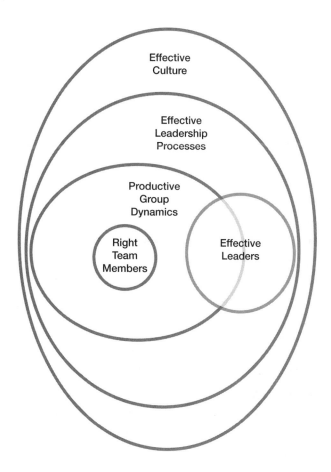

FIGURE 8: *Elements of an effective organization*

"So, let me ask this question, Sol: if I cover all of those elements am I assured I'll have a high performing team?"

"Ah, good question, Dean. You can do your part, which is huge, but you really need to step back and look at the whole organization. Research has shown that you can distill an effective organization down to five elements: effective leaders, an effective leadership process, productive group dynamics, the right team members, and an effective culture.

"You also need to keep in mind a few things we've learned from the field of evolutionary psychology. If you observe primitive tribes, you will see that leadership is needed—and desired—only in times of scarcity. In times of abundance, no one wants to be led. They just want to be happy where they are. In times of scarcity, people will look for someone to aid them, to lead them out of their difficulty. We are no different today. In good times we complain that we are being micromanaged, or led, when we feel that we don't need to be. In difficult times we look to a leader to provide direction for us. That's the vision. Now, having heard this you can understand why an unethical leader might invent a crisis—so that individuals will look to their leader to guide them to safety. Essentially you have an ego-driven crisis."

"Hmm, that makes a lot of sense," Dean responded. "I just wonder how many people have died in wars these so-called leaders created."

"Yes, it's quite sad, Dean. You're on the right track. Now add to those crises ones driven by the strongest drive we human beings have—the drive to eat and procreate—and you begin to understand why we've had so many wars. So, if you step back and think about these powerful forces, at their deepest level they are acting on our physical bodies to keep our species alive. That's what programmed them into our DNA in the first place."

"Wow, I'd never thought of that before, but it sure makes sense. But, how does this relate to your leadership model."

"Ah, thank you for keeping me on task," Sol said with a smile. "What is really important is the leadership process. It doesn't matter who carries out the process—a designated leader or individuals on the team—it just matters that the work is done. If almost everyone on a team can be a leader for some aspect of the task at hand, then a single central leader may not be necessary, and in fact may be counterproductive."

"I don't get it, Sol. It seems to me that you have to have a leader."

"No, not necessarily, Dean. It's called distributed leadership. It can be done quite well by mature teams, those who have been in existence for a long time. And so, the reason I brought up this idea of evolutionary psychology is that if a team is self-led, or self-managed, they get to choose how much leadership they need at any given moment."

Dean shifted in his chair and thought for a moment, "Hmm, I'll have to think about that one some more. I do have one more question, Sol. You've talked about people leaving an organization if they're not satisfied, but I frequently hear about people staying in organizations where there are abusive relationships and horrible work environments. Why would they do that?"

"Dean, you have to understand why people work. I've found that it's usually for one of two reasons—either people need money or they want to fulfill a need to be useful and provide meaning to their life. Now remember the two fundamental worker aspects—job performance and job satisfaction.

"Let's look at the people who work for money first. For these folks, who are the large majority of workers, they will perform in their job out of fear, fear of losing their job. And—they may stay in a job that they are not satisfied with simply because they need money to pay for food, housing, healthcare, etc. So these people will put up with poor leadership, poor management, abuse, and so on, just to keep their paycheck coming. This is what leads to worker exploitation and the growth of unions. But overall, we've found from research that if people are not satisfied with their jobs they're more likely to leave or miss work more often.

"Now let's look at the people who work because it brings meaning to their lives. Clearly, if they are not satisfied in their job they'll simply leave. They're not tied to their job because of a paycheck. It comes back to that intrinsic motivation element. Does that help?"

"Yeah, it does. It also helps explain why people hunker down and stay put in a job during times of downsizing and recessions, but once the economy starts to pick up the good ones start moving around. That brings a lot of clarity to it. Thanks, Sol."

"No problem, my good man. No problem. So where is your project at the moment?"

Still pondering all that Sol had said, Dean pulled his car into a spot near the DandaData entrance. Glancing at his watch, he thought, *4:30, good. I can get another hour of work done and then it's onto the weekend for me.* Heaving the car door open, the sun filtered onto the side of the door, and Dean squinted as the blast of light hit his face. He grabbed his notebook, locked the door, and headed for the entrance. *Ah, this bright sun and warm June air feels wonderful. I must be crazy to be going back inside. With the summer solstice nearing, at least we've got lots of light during the day. Hmm, who is this heading my way? Appears to be Anton's lanky form...*

"Hey Dean! I've got to pick up a kid from soccer."

"Uh, sure, no problem Anton. Have a great—" Dean stopped as he saw Anton's face turn into an ugly frown.

"Dean, there's something I really need to talk to you about.

Look, can we sit down together on Monday?"

"Yeah, sure... We've got the staff meeting at 9:00, can you come in and talk around 8:00?"

Anton's face softened. "Yeah... yeah. I think that would be good." He hesitated, appearing ready to speak again, but no words came forth. And then a blank look came over his face.

"Is there something you want to say right now?"

"No, no..." Nodding his head, Anton continued in a flat voice, "I'll compose my thoughts more over the weekend, and we can talk on Monday morning. Thanks, Dean."

Turning away before he could respond, Dean was left watching Anton's deliberate steps toward his car. *Sheesh, great, now I've got to wait all weekend to find out what's bugging him. Damn! Maybe I'll just head home, too...*

chapter five

The life-force of the universe is a relentless energy, moving ever forward without hesitation. Hop on and enjoy the ride!

Eight o'clock and no Anton... Hmm. I wonder what the heck is eating at him. I guess I'll review my notes for the staff meeting at nine. Oh I just want to get this over with...

Knock, knock, came the rap on his open door.

Startled, Dean jumped in his chair, his head snapping toward the door. "Oh hi, Anton. How was your weekend," he said calmly, belying the nervousness in his belly.

"Hey, Dean. It was good. Thanks for meeting with me." Motioning toward the door, Anton asked, "Is it OK if I close the door?"

"Sure, and have a seat."

"Look, Dean, I know that we've been together a long time and have worked closely on the NU technology, and don't get me wrong, I've enjoyed it, and continue to enjoy it, but, well, I've been looking at other opportunities and am wondering if I shouldn't be somewhere else."

Damn, this is not what I need. He's my key guy. "Like where?"

"For example, I still have family back in Russia, and they don't know much about NU technology there. I could be a hero, an icon in my old country. Even though I wasn't born there, I speak the language fluently and have a lot of connections. I just... wanted to... talk to you about it..."

Dean let Anton's statement sink in for a few moments before responding. *I wonder what his motive is here. What does he really want?* "Anton, can you help me out? What is it that you're trying to tell me? Are you unhappy here and want to leave, or are you just exploring new opportunities for yourself? In other words, are you feeling a push to leave or a pull to explore more opportunities?"

Hesitating, Anton looked up and took a deep breath. "Look Dean, you and I go way back, we've worked together a lot over the years, and I don't think it's fair that you've gotten this job and I didn't. You and I both know that I know more about this technology than you do. So what gives? Why am I working for you? It should be the other way around."

Dean's heart raced and he looked Anton straight in the eye. He thought for a moment, wanting the tension to diffuse. Calmed, he recalled the communication skill he had learned in a college psychology class to resolve conflict. "So Anton, what you're saying is that you feel you know the NU technology better than I and that our roles should be switched, that I should be working for you? Is that correct?"

"Yeah, you know Dean, it just doesn't seem fair. I've worked hard on this technology, I've given DandaData a lot of my time and effort, and it just doesn't seem to be getting me very far. Maybe I could do better elsewhere. You know as well as I do that people who move around a lot tend to move up their career ladders faster." Anton's body began to tense, his energy building, "Why should I stay here? Can you give me a good reason? It just doesn't seem fair Dean. I mean—. Oh, never mind."

"No, go on."

Anton hesitated, looked to the side then snapped back, pressing his pointed finger into the table, his knuckle turning white. "Damn it, Dean, I mean, this really sucks. I'm tired of this shit. I'm tired of being number two on the team! Fu—. Arrgh!" He shook his head like a lion. "It's bullshit, that's what it is, bullshit."

Whoa, now what do I do? Ooh, his face is even turning red. Mmm, I wonder how I can get him to look inward, more deeply. "Hang on Anton, hang on. I understand you're frustrated, so let's see how we can work through this. So what you're saying is that you're tired of being number two and that you'd like to move up in your career more quickly? Is that correct?"

"Yeah, that's what I'm saying. Can't you figure that out? Geez, Dean, we've worked together a long time and I thought you were a smart guy..."

Now what did Sol say about that motivation and hygiene stuff? Man, I feel like I'm taking a quiz already, and he just told me about this stuff on Friday. Only problem is that I don't just get a grade, my project can go down the tubes if I can't salvage this. Oh, what a pain... "Anton, so it seems that we've got several issues here, or is it just one? Is the central issue that you feel you're not moving up quickly enough or that you're upset because you feel that I'm moving up and you're not?"

The questions gave Anton pause as he leaned back and considered them. The tension began to diffuse but then a quizzical expression grew across Anton's face. "What do you mean? What are you asking, Dean? I don't know that I get it."

"Anton, what I'm trying to do is to get at the heart of the issue or issues. I know that you're frustrated and I want to work together with you to resolve this. You know from many of our past discussions that I value your knowledge and the way that you can conceptualize how to adapt and use a given technology to solve a particularly thorny problem. You're right. I can't do that as well as you. Now, can you pinpoint what the deepest issue is for you? Is it that you just feel frustrated you're not moving as quickly in your career or that you feel you've not been treated fairly regarding your advancement versus mine or something even different from that?"

Anton's jaw was clenched, pushing it to one side as he pondered. With a blank look he peered ahead. "Hmm, well, I don't know Dean. I mean, yeah, I'm clearly frustrated, and you ask a damn good question. And it's one that I've not really considered. I guess I get so frustrated that I can't seem to see what the heart of the matter is."

"Yeah, I understand that, Anton. I get that way sometimes, too. I guess when it happens to me I try to sit back and think about how I feel and ask myself, 'Why do I feel this way?' It sometimes takes me a while, but I usually figure it out." *Let me see if I've got this stuff figured out...*

"Look Anton, I want you to be happy here, to stay and help us finish the project. You are clearly our key guy on the NU technology. I also want to leave you with a thought. You know better than I that we've got some tremendous challenges to completing this project. You've got some outstanding ideas for ways that we can jump ahead of BenSoft with NU technology. You know the problems we don't know how to solve. Just think, if you wait for another year, work on those problems and solve them, you'd get industry recognition for doing so. Wouldn't that be quite an achievement and something you could point to, to show others what you've done? Think about it, Anton."

Anton looked up at Dean, his head resting on a more relaxed body. "OK, Dean. You do bring up some good points. Let me think about it more. Hey, I'm sorry I got upset with you, Dean. But you've given me some food for thought."

"Alright, good. Anton, listen, once again, I want you to know that you are a key guy on this project and that I think you could make some stellar contributions to it. Can we follow up on this conversation in, say a week or a week and a half?"

"Yeah, sure. It'll give me some time to think about it." Gazing directly at Dean, he said, "Thanks Dean."

"Oh, and Anton, I know each of you talk about your teams at the staff meetings, but maybe you can tell me a bit more about how yours is working right now."

"Sure. We're actually doing really well. Rick and Stacy have already solved a couple of the thorny technical issues. We still have that device discovery problem to get fixed, though. Ya know, now that you mention it, it's turned out really well that we have someone with marketing experience on our team. Sally pointed out how much mileage we can get in the marketplace with just a couple of our new networking features. They're actually simple things for us to include, but it sounds like they will be important features for the customers. And so far everyone has been really open about new ideas and ways to get the product out the door on a short timetable. Is that what you're looking for, Dean?"

"Yep, that's exactly what I'm looking for. So what are your biggest problems in the team right now?"

Anton took a deep breath and thought for a moment. "Dean, I guess the biggest problem we have right now is just the massive amount of work ahead. We need to stay focused on getting the coding done and making sure it's good code. We're also having a bit of trouble with Tony's group. We can't get them focused on putting the hooks in their code for the NU technology. Why do you ask? Are you concerned about the team?"

"I just like to know how it's going, wanting to know if all the issues that need to be addressed are being addressed."

Anton's voice became softer, more gentle. "No, I think we're doing remarkably well, Dean. I think we're OK."

As Anton rose to leave, Dean perceived him to be slightly different than when he had come in. *Hopefully he'll be able to look inside himself, to discover what is there. Hopefully he'll stay...*

Dean smiled as he watched the animated discussions among the team leaders. Raising his voice to be heard about the din, he began, "Let's get this staff meeting going. Welcome everyone. I hope you've had a good weekend, and I thank all of you for being here this week after the Fourth of July.

"The first thing we need to do is to get Advay and Priya on the phone for a status. Can someone get them on the speakerphone?"

Dean began, "Advay, we've got Team Alpha in the room here, and we'd like to get a brief status. Who do you have on the line over there?"

"It's just Priya and me here, Dean."

"Sounds good. So, can you give us an update?"

"Sure, and we have good news for you folks. As of late last week, our team here in India is now fully staffed. We can begin doing the work with full force."

"Excellent news, Advay. Congratulations!"

"Thank you. We're very happy about it as well. So in the coming weeks we will be giving you an update on our progress."

"Great, great."

"That's all we have, Dean. Do you have anything else for us?"

"Nope, that's good enough for us today. Thanks again," Dean said as the phone was disconnected.

Turning to address the local team, Dean continued, "Wow, that's a nice achievement for them. Now I'd like to remind everyone of our goals that we've agreed to with Jim and Tony. We have the timelines with the full function and GA dates, of course, but we also have the agreement that we're not adding any new function, just the NU technology and its associated installation and maintenance improvements. Now, if you guys feel that it's easy to slip something in because of what we need to change to add NU, then that's OK—if you don't impact the schedule.

"Any questions?" as Dean scanned the room.

Anton raised his hand and began to speak. "Dean, it's interesting that you should mention the agreement with Jim and Tony because, as I mentioned earlier, several of us are having more and more problems with Tony's teams. First off, they're not very open to helping us get hooks into their code to enable NU technology. They seem to be dragging their feet on this. Then, to make matters worse, they are putting some new features in that they claim have been requested by one of our big customers. They say it won't affect the schedule, but we all know that it will add risk."

"Dean, my team has been working with Anton's on this and he's right, this really is getting to be a problem," Sarah added. "I think I can speak for everyone in this room by saying that all of us try to work together to create a good product. For example, just the other day two of my guys sat down with Mark Floransia from Anton's team and figured out how to get past a problem displaying the discovered devices. We're working this stuff out, Dean. We're trying to get it done but Tony's group is really putting up roadblocks."

Dean looked down at his notes and drummed his thumb on the desk. Looking up, he replied, "So Tony's really not in alignment here—with either us or Jim." Shaking his head, he continued, "Let me think a bit about what might be the best way to handle this. Sarah and Anton, can we meet at nine in the morning in my office?"

"Sure."

"Yeah, I can do that."

"Sounds good. I'll probably need to talk to Tony, and then based on the outcome of that meeting I need to decide whether or not to bring Randy into it."

"Tony, thanks for taking the time to meet with me. As I indicated when we talked briefly, I'd like to talk about the alignment of our goals for Project Phoenix," Dean began. "My understanding from Jim is that we are to have the product available for a GA of July 23rd next year, that we are supposed to incorporate the NU technology for enhanced installation and maintenance capability, and beyond that we are to add no new features. Is that your understanding?"

Tony remained upright in his chair, popping his gum and staring straight at Dean. Finally he said, "Dean, I hear what you're saying, but you don't understand. I've had MozArCo asking us to add the remote folder viewing for two years now. You know how big a customer they are. I've been telling them that we'll eventually get that feature into the code for a long time. I'd be pretty embarrassed to plop out a new version of code without that feature."

Looking aside and then turning back, Dean replied, "Tony, I agree with you that MozArCo is an important customer of ours, but first off, what if we fall behind because of your added feature? Then how will you look to Jim?"

"Aw Dean, you worry too much. I told my guys to make it happen, and they'll do it. Don't worry. Listen, you remember what I told you? You've got to take charge. I know that you're new at this stuff, so take it from a guy like me who's been around the block a few times. I know what to do. You could learn a thing or two from me."

When Dean closed his eyes Tony's popping gum sounded as if it were filling the room. Open eyes were better. This meant he had to look at Tony, but at least the popping noises were less intrusive. "Yes, I certainly respect all the work you've done, Tony, but I'd like to get back to the issue at hand. Let me shift gears for a moment. Have your guys talked to you about incorporating NU technology in your code base?"

"Well sure. They tell me what's going on all of the time. Why do you ask?"

"From what my team leads are telling me it sounds as if there may be difficulty adding the hooks for NU technology in your code. Have you heard anything about this? If it's true, we've got to have our guys working intimately together to get the problems hashed out now before it becomes a big problem."

Tony remained stiff. "I know that they're working on it, Dean, but you know that the burden to get the NU technology in our product is your responsibility, not mine."

Great. Now he's trying to crater the schedule and blame it on me. Now I understand his game... Dean straightened his body and took a deep, audible breath. "OK, Tony, I get the message. How 'bout this: if I come back to you with some specific problem areas where we are having difficulty integrating the NU technology into the existing code base, will you agree to look into it?"

"Absolutely, Dean! You know I'm here to help, to make this project a success. I would definitely look into it for you. So what else can I do for you today?"

"That's it. Nothing else really. Thanks for your time, Tony. Once again, I appreciate it."

"No problem. Let's stay in touch," Tony replied as Dean rose to his feet.

"Yeah, let's stay in touch," Dean muttered, placing his hand on the door lever. He hesitated for an instant, uncertain whether to speak more or not. His senses heightened, Dean took in the swirled brown tones of the wood door, the brushed stainless steel handle in his hand, and the short industrial blue carpet. Deciding there was nothing to be gained with more words, he pressed the lever and tugged at the door. Without looking back Dean entered the hallway, feeling as if he were able to finally catch a full breath, the repression lifted.

The visits began to feel familiar, yet Dean continued to get an other-world sense when he met with Sol. The connection was strong and Sol's presence palpable to Dean.

"Sol, I'm really starting to get worried about the project. We're not progressing as quickly as we should be. Do you have any ideas that might be helpful?"

"Let me ask you a question. Do you have milestones and goals in place to quantitatively measure your progress? I think we talked about that before."

"Of course we do, but they're spaced pretty far apart. Why?"

"Because you need to know at any given time how well your project is doing. There is a model that you might be interested in. Many years ago some researchers observed activities in several teams as they moved through a specific task. The researchers noticed that the activities in each team roughly fit the same pattern—they got off to a slow start and then about halfway through realized that they would not reach their goal unless something changed. At this point they re-evaluated their plan and progress, created a new plan, and then worked to meet their goal. They called the model the punctuated equilibrium model.

"It's really similar to what people often call a midlife crisis. At the halfway mark, people start looking farther forward instead of backward, at the present moment, or incremental steps forward. What this means for you is that you've got to break your project down into reasonably small chunks so that you will know very quickly if you're running into trouble rather than waiting until the halfway mark to find out."

"Hmm, I see. That makes sense. We certainly can break the project down into smaller tasks. Part of the problem is that some of the team is in India, and I really don't know how well they're progressing. They keep saying they're doing well, but they aren't asking many questions. I have a suspicion that they're not really very far along and won't admit it."

"That certainly sounds like a possibility. We call those teams where some members are not located in the same physical location as others, 'virtual teams.' One of the problems with such teams is that they feel disconnected. The element of trust takes more effort to build. When other members of your team are from a different country, there is also a culture gap you must bridge. When was the last time you visited them?"

"That's part of the problem, too—I've never visited them. One of the other managers has been over there a few times, but all of us have not gotten together since our teams have joined."

Stroking his beard once again, Sol pondered a response. "Dean, you have to realize the importance of just walking around and chatting with your team members, emotionally 'touching' them, making a connection."

"If I did that wouldn't they think I'm just goofing off, just having a little stroll instead of really working?"

"Ah, quite the contrary, Dean. After all, we are human beings, mammals in our DNA. Deep down we all need that human connection, that emotional touch. That's what's so special about charismatic leadership. If you make that connection with people, make them feel that they are important enough to you that you'll spend at least a few minutes getting to know them and find out what they're passionate about, you will create a bond with that person and they will follow you. That's the sign of a true leader.

"Forget about that list of characteristics we came up with at our first meeting. If you simply acknowledge to your people that you genuinely value them as contributors to your team and focus them on the goal, they will produce for you. Leadership is about focus. Focus on the goal, focus on the people getting the work done and everything else falls into place."

Dean sat back and smiled, "I think you've mentioned this a time or two, Sol. Maybe it will eventually sink in. Focus. I've got to remember to focus so that I can make my goal."

Sol's head jerked up to stare at Dean. "Dean, did you say *my* goal?"

"Yeah, why?" *Oops, I think I blew that one! I wonder why the stare.*

"Dean, one characteristic of a good leader is that he or she will talk about the plural—we, our, and not I or my. Let's talk about what I call the 'ego spectrum.' I created a spectrum for ego involvement in our daily activities. Keep in mind that our ego is our identity, or our sense of self. You can think of each place on the spectrum as being about your ego orientation to the outer world. At one end, we have what I call self-importance. This is about individuals who think primarily about themselves. To them, they are the only people who really matter. These people may have been hurt at some time in the past and have become closed off to others or may be that way by nature. As we move to the next orientation of our ego, we get to pride. If we become too proud of our achievements we can easily slip into an inflated sense of self-worth and once again close ourself off from others. Reaching to the other end of the scale we find humility. Here we have no ego."

"Oh, sort of like the monk living in the cave? I would think that he doesn't have an ego. He's just waiting for someone to bring him food each day!"

Sol hesitated. "Yes... I guess you could put it that way. Sure... So the monk is purposely setting his ego aside to let the world continue

FIGURE 9. *Healthy ego spectrum*

on around him without his involvement. Let me ask you: if you have total humility and set your ego, or your identity, aside completely, how would you lead your team?"

"Hmm. That's a hard question. It's sort of like, how can I lead while sitting in the cave all day every day. I don't know, it doesn't seem like it would work."

"Correct. It won't really work. If you set your ego aside you will not be adding any of your energy toward the goal. Essentially you are abdicating your position as a leader. So let's go on to the last ego orientation—confidence, or a healthy ego. Here you are using your sense of value, your sense of self to move your project and team forward yet not becoming absorbed in your particular involvement. It's a delicate sense of balance. In this orientation you are using your ego to work closely with your team, your peers, and your superiors to ensure everyone is working together toward the same goal. Think of it more as guiding rather than prodding or pushing. Does this make sense, Dean?"

"Yes... but... you seemed to have quite a reaction a few minutes ago when I said *my* goal. Can I ask what that was about?"

Stern and composed, Sol once again looked directly at Dean. "Let me ask you this, when you say *my* goal rather than *our* goal, which of these ego orientations do you think you are closer to?"

"Hmm, well, now that you mention it, I guess pride or self-importance."

"Yes, exactly, and that's why I had such a strong reaction to it. If you want to become a true leader, Dean, you will need to observe yourself and see if you can determine where you are on that scale. If you say *our* instead of *my*, you are including yourself, or having confidence in yourself as well as including others. This is a healthy way to use your ego."

"This definitely gives me something to think about, but is there some way I can figure out how I'm doing?"

"Good question, Dean, and one I wish more folks would ask. I frequently work with leaders who are not able to observe their behavior and therefore don't have a good understanding of the effect they have on their team. Several people have worked to create assessments of what is called 'mindfulness,' or the ability to objectively observe our own reaction to the present moment. If we can work on observing our reactions, we likely become more aware of our behavior and how our ego is affecting that behavior. It can truly be a transformational experience. Does that help provide a structure for you?

"Yes... yes it does, but wow, seems like that will take a lot of effort."

"Yes, it will take some effort, but I think you'll find that the experience is well worth it. It's helpful to always maintain a positive attitude toward self-development, Dean. Just as individuals should be looking to improve, teams should as well. In fact research has shown that teams who are vigilant about staying aware of the latest technology and have a self-development orientation can remain productive for many years. They don't get stale and need an infusion of 'new blood' as some like to say. You need to take the time to regroup, sit back and think about where you're going. Sometimes you just need to enter the stillness as an individual or even as a team."

Dean sat quietly, allowing the thought to settle in while Sol embraced the quiet of the moment, practicing what he had just preached. Dean looked directly at Sol. "So, it really doesn't have to take a lot of effort, I don't really have to work hard at it? I guess when I really think about it, it just sort of... flows?"

"That's right... it just flows."

The conversation ebbed and a stillness entered the space. It was in this moment that Dean and Sol's world stopped. They were indeed sitting in Sol's office, the bird songs and student voices continued to flow, but in that instant they were in a different space, in a different dimension. Dean could sense a shift in consciousness, a feeling of expansion beyond the four walls of Sol's office. His breath was energetic, as if every molecule in the vicinity was rising and falling with each inhalation and exhalation.

"Dean, what is important to realize is that the universe is really very simple. At the heart there is an energy that just moves forward, it wants to progress. Imagine you are in a river. If you grab onto a branch along the side, you'll be fighting and struggling to hang on, trying to control where you go. This takes a lot of effort. However, if you have the courage to let go of that branch anchoring you to the shore, you can allow yourself to merge into the middle of the stream and swiftly move forward. You may think that you are out of control, and you are somewhat, but guess what—at least you're moving forward. You're making progress. And as you are cruising down this flowing stream, you can paddle to the left or to the right, and so you do have some measure of control.

"Now think about how much less effort this takes than trying to hold onto that branch. Allow yourself to flow with the energy of your team. Imagine the flow of each member's energy as their own individual river. Now gently guide their flow toward the goal. Every single person on this planet has an energetic flow moving forward. Athletes call it 'being in the zone.' It's the same thing. Your job as the leader is to nudge and guide that energy toward the goal. Focus. Focus that energy toward the goal, and your job is done.

"That doesn't mean that you're not going to have problems, that there won't be ripples along the way, because those things will happen. And when they do, you don't have to make it difficult. Just focus on the goal and how the energy must be directed toward the goal, and everything else will fall into place."

Silence once again filled the space, and Dean felt both full and empty. He felt expansive, filled with this new idea of energy in leadership, yet empty because there was nothing for him to grab on to. *Just get into the flow?*

Sol rose from his chair, startling Dean back into the material world. "Don't think about this, Dean. Feel it, just feel it. I'm sorry, but I've really got to get to this class, or I'm going to have a bunch of cranky grad students flowing down the wrong river. Dean, I also want you to know that I'm really beginning to enjoy these discussions we've had... I look forward to many more of them. It's been enjoyable watching you grow into this new leadership role. Thanks for that."

As Dean emerged from the building he felt confused, unsure what to do next. There was one thing he did know that he wanted to do, though, and that was to savor this moment, a moment when everything seemed to be exactly as it should be. He didn't feel himself walking to his car, he flowed to his car. Everything external to him appeared as a play, a drama on a stage. *I do know one thing, I think I need to head to India. Sol has been an incredible help to me. He's right, I've really grown through just these four interactions. I can't imagine what I'll learn in the next four interactions.*

"Hey, Dean, thanks for taking the time to talk with me again," Anton said. "Ya know, Dean, we've talked twice now since I got so upset with you, and I want you to know that you've asked me some really good questions, some really tough questions. And I appreciate that."

Anton was relaxed. His body seemed to melt into the chair, allowing it to mold his body.

"Anton, I definitely appreciate you sharing your thoughts," Dean replied, leaving silence for Anton to speak again.

"As I've thought about your questions more, I guess I've realized that I was jealous that you were picked as our manager and now you've gotten a much bigger role in Project Phoenix than I have. That didn't sit well with me because I felt that I deserved at least the same treatment as you. I mean, we started on this project together, Dean.

"It's hard for me to say this, Dean, but after you asked me some of those questions at the beginning of these conversations I've come to realize that you truly built a good team. The guys we've got on our team are open to new ideas and eager to go implement them. That's a real tribute to you. When I look at myself, I see that I wouldn't have brought in the type of folks that you did. I probably would have brought in only the hard core techie types. But now you've shown me the wisdom of diversity. As I said... it's hard for me to say this, Dean, but I really think you've done a good job, and I can honestly say that I'm proud to be a member of Team Alpha."

"Wow, thanks for the nice words and thoughts, Anton." The words allowed Dean to relax. "So, given what you've just told me, what are your thoughts regarding moving on to somewhere else?"

"I've thought a lot about that, too, Dean, and you're right. I need to finish this project and then see where that takes me. Maybe there will be something good for me here, and maybe not. But for now, I'm staying right here and on the project."

Dean simply looked at Anton and smiled, allowing the words to steep.

"I really don't know what to say, Anton, other than to say that I'm delighted that you want to stay and that, again, I appreciate the kind words and thoughts. It's guys like you that make this job rewarding. It seems that your team is hitting on all cylinders and that's a real testament to the leadership you've provided. So thank you for that... Is there anything else?"

Anton didn't budge. He seemed so comfortable in that chair in Dean's office that it appeared that he could stay all day. *Hmmm, it looks like Anton is definitely in a different spot emotionally than he was a month and a half ago when he came in spewing his anger and frustration. It's almost like he's in another world.*

"No, no, I think that's it..." Anton finally leaned forward and then smiled at Dean. He hoisted his loose body from the chair and added, "Well, I'll see you in a few minutes at the staff meeting, Dean. Thanks again."

What a way to start a week...

Dean arrived at Tony's office, finding he and Becky already engaged in conversation. Startled at Dean's appearance, Becky looked up. "Oh... hey Dean. We were just about to get started," she said, her voice shaking.

Hmm, I wonder what that's about...

"You ready to chat about the India team?" Tony began.

"Yeah, I'm starting to get worried about their progress," Dean stated as he plopped into a chair.

Tony said, "I know that you've given them a schedule that is three weeks ahead of ours so that we have a buffer, but it seems that we don't have enough information from them to really determine where they are. What do you think?"

Dean replied, "I agree. Look, this project is so important that I've been wondering if we shouldn't just go over there and investigate. Becky, you know these guys better than both of us. What do you think?"

"My experience has been that it's sometimes difficult to figure out where they are on a project and then the last week they start asking a lot of questions. It seems like they don't do much work and then as the deadline approaches there is a flurry of activity. They frequently miss deadlines. I have found that going over there certainly helps, and given the critical nature of this project, it wouldn't be a bad idea."

"So who should go?" Tony asked.

"Maybe you and I should go, Dean," Becky suggested. "I know these folks well, and they'll probably enjoy seeing a familiar face. You know the project well, and Tony has the majority of the team to deal with here so maybe he should stay. What do you think?"

"I hate to take the time away from here, but, yeah, I guess that makes sense," Dean replied. *I really hate to leave Tony here mind-*

ing the store, though. No telling what trouble he's going to cook up.

"OK, but one thing to make sure of Dean: when you review the schedule that you use their project schedule, not ours," Tony said.

"Tony, you know that I don't agree with that, but I'll do it because you asked. Just remember, it's your idea and not mine. I'll let Advay know we're coming."

Becky chirped up, "Dean, it really should be great fun, too. Don't worry, I've been there three times. I'll show you around."

"Thanks, Becky. OK, sounds like a plan, then," Dean said, as Becky's eyes flashed a hard glance at him.

chapter six

*A lie repeated a hundred times becomes
the truth.* —CHAIRMAN MAO

Bong, the bell sounded as the plane jerked to a halt. Despite
his sleep-deprived state, Dean sprang into the aisle in order to
claim space.

"It has been a pleasure serving you on your flight to Bengaluru.
We hope that you have enjoyed your flight on Air India and ask
that you consider flying with us on your next trip. Thank you
and have a pleasant and safe rest of your journey."

"Mmm, it feels good to stretch my legs again. Becky, looks
like you're having a hard time waking up."

"Oh man, what time is it? I mean what time is it Michigan
time?" Her limp body was plastered to the side of the plane.

"Let's see, it's 6:20 p.m. You've still got the whole evening to
go. You should be wide awake." Dean smiled at her grogginess.

"Ugh, but didn't I miss something, like a whole night's worth of sleep? So what time is it India time?" she said, still clasping the pillow.

"Well, let's see, if I can do my calculations correctly... Uh, I'm going to say that it's 4:50 a.m."

"Oh my God, this is insane. OK... OK... I guess I'll get up. I really don't want to stay in this damn plane any longer than I have to." Reaching her arm over the empty seat in front of her, Becky hoisted her tired body upright to stand in between the two rows of seats. Looking around, it appeared to Becky as if a tornado had traversed the entire length of the plane. Magazines and newspapers littered the floor. Headsets dangled from seat pockets; pillows and blankets were strewn everywhere. "Dean, is this the same plane we got on when we started? The one we got on had everything arranged in such order. Look at it now! Amazing. What a mess."

Searching in the overhead bin, Dean asked, "What color is your briefcase? Is it this beige one?"

Trying to talk while yawning, "Hmm, yeah, that's the one."

"Here you go. C'mon, the line is starting to move."

"Aw geez, let's see, my book, jacket, and my iPod. I think that's it... Oh, thanks for letting me out, Dean."

"No problem. Off to a new adventure! Here we come."

Becky glanced back as she began to move forward. "How in the world can you remain so chipper?"

"I don't know, I just do it, I guess."

Upon entering the jetway, Dean felt like he was hitting a wall of heat and humidity. "Argh, this humidity is really oppressive."

"Don't worry about it. I've found that you get used to it pretty quickly. Now who's whining?"

"OK, OK."

Emerging into the concourse, Dean squinted in the bright lights of the ultra-modern terminal. "Wow, Becky, you didn't tell me India was like this. This is a real let-down. I had visions of walking off the jetway into some mystical place. After studying Eastern philosophy for many years, I had the impression that India was a magical land. This could be anywhere in the world. In fact it's better than most any airport in the world. What's next?"

"Well, we need to get through immigration and customs. C'mon, let's go... I'm starting to wake up now..."

"I don't know if that's a blessing or not," Dean said, enjoying the casual teasing. "I guess I'll just follow you."

Dean straggled behind Becky, which allowed him to relax a bit and settle his nervousness. His mind was turning over the challenge ahead. *I sure hope we can get this team back on track. I wonder if these folks are up to the task. I hope I don't get sick. How in the heck do we check into a hotel at 5:00 in the morning?* As Dean made his way through the customs and immigration process, he calmed a bit, able to soak in the surroundings. *Hmm, I may be a minority here, but oddly I don't feel out of place. No one's staring at me. That's a good sign.*

As their air conditioned taxi wheeled onto the dusty highway, Dean began to get a feel for the real India. The four-lane ribbon of concrete appeared without a single lane marking. Cars seemed to travel aimlessly down the highway, careening from side to side as they passed slower moving vehicles. Dean's mind wandered to Sol's story of allowing the energy to move us forward, as if down a river.

The dusty yet generous shoulder appeared to be a way station for all sorts of vendors, travelers, and tent dwellers. And then there were the cows. Every now and then a cow or two would be seen scouring the trash for a morsel or eyeing the automobiles seemingly without a care in the world.

In the pre-dawn hours, the city had not yet come alive, yet a sprinkling of people were boarding buses toward the center of town, heading for an early work day. While the highway was an integral component of the Bengaluru infrastructure, it seemed to be an organism of its own, having its own ecosystem. Food appeared to be available from ramshackle stands amongst auto repair stalls, sketchy retail outlets, and a wide assortment of street vendors.

"Becky, I don't understand this. How can this incredible contrast exist? We just walked off a state-of-the-art airliner, through an ultra-modern airport, and now we're speeding down a highway seeing people sleeping on the streets. How can this be?"

"You haven't seen anything yet, Dean. Wait until we get to the hotel."

"Looks like this is going to be an interesting trip... You know, my impressions of India come from my Eastern philosophy and religion studies. Seems I had this vision of India as being this mystical, sacred place. Uh, this seems quite a bit different from that."

As the early light of dawn became apparent, the taxi turned off the highway onto a narrow city street. Three-wheeled auto rickshaws littered the pavement. Some idled by the side of the road, awaiting a new day and a few rupees to transport someone from one part of the city to another. Others slowly coughed their way down the street, like sluggish insects for the taxi to overcome. Nestled amidst the lush foliage and aging office buildings, the hotel driveway appeared. The taxi made a sharp right turn into the hotel driveway and pulled under a generous awning. Dean peered out the window to discover yet another contrast—a five star marble-clad hotel with an x-ray scanner and a walk-through metal detector just like at the airport. Before Dean could process this dichotomy, a large man in a white formal uniform complete with turban was upon the car, his hand firmly clutching the door handle, pulling with a force that could have ripped the door off a bank vault.

"Good morning sir. Welcome to our hotel. Don't worry about your bags. We will deliver them to your room. Don't worry about a thing. We will take care of everything. Please come this way. Come, come," he said, as he motioned Dean out of the taxi.

Looking behind for Becky, Dean saw that her own personal manservant was providing identical service.

Lagging to allow her to catch up, Dean muttered, "Now I think I'm getting a sense of what you're talking about. We just came off a dusty, filthy road—into this. Wow. What else?"

"Oh, you'll see," as she flashed a broad smile. "Wait until you see the lobby. These folks know how to do it right."

Dean and Becky trudged up the massive brown steps and placed their personal bags on the conveyor belt. As Dean walked through the metal detector a shrill beep alerted the attendant. The man operating the conveyor rushed out and waved Dean on through, "Come, come. It's no problem, come, come."

"Uh..." as he looked back at Becky.

"Shh, just keep walking. Trust me," as she shoved him forward. "You'll learn."

So why all of this gear if they're not even going to use it? Sheesh... Dean grabbed his bag which was now sitting at the end of the conveyor while the supposed security agent motioned them toward the lobby door. "Come, come this way. Come, please. Enjoy your stay."

When they approached the expansive glass doors, the two doormen opened them on cue as if an automatic signal had been triggered. Looking ahead into the lobby, Dean now understood what Becky had been alluding to. Smack in the middle of the enormous lobby sat an equally enormous arrangement of cut flowers, most of a kind he had never seen before. The size and color made them seem other-worldly. He could not imagine how heavy the vase was. For a moment he thought he might be able to crawl inside it.

Prying his eyes from the flowers he began to take in the remainder of the lobby. Brown marble continued the exterior theme. Everywhere he looked, the only word that came to mind was elegant. From the fine oriental rugs to the velvet-covered sofas, to the delicate light fixtures and stone mosaic accents on the walls, every appointment was first class.

"Now I've got it. Wow, these folks sure do know how to do it right. I can't imagine what this cost."

"Less than you'd imagine, I'll tell you that. Sometimes it's amazing what you can get things for here. C'mon, I want to get to my room, shower, and get some clean clothes on. The desk is over there."

As Becky approached the counter a smartly dressed woman leaned forward and asked, "Welcome to our hotel. May I help you?"

"Yes, my name is Rebecca Green. I should have a reservation."

"Just a minute please while I check..."

I think I just might like this place after all. Yeah, I think I will.

"Excuse me sir, may I help you? Do you have a reservation?"

"Huh, oh, uh, yes. Uh, I'm Dean Edmonds."

"Just a minute please while I look up your reservation. I'm sure it's in here..."

Becky waved her key card at Dean to get his attention. "Hey Dean, we're supposed to be at the office around nine. The drive will take us about 45 minutes, and we'll need to stop and get a bite to eat on the way, so we should probably meet down here about 7:45. How does that sound?"

"Sounds good to me. Where are we eating?"

"Oh, just a sidewalk café," she exclaimed. Becky flashed another smile, "You'll see. It's very local."

"I hope it's good. See you then." *Wow—good accommodations, good company. I think I'm going to like this trip just fine...*

Dean peered out the taxi window. *If I just rolled the window down, I could reach out and touch these folks in the auto rickshaw next to me.* The two women in the auto sat lifeless, staring forward and leaning into each other. The older woman, whom Dean guessed to be the mother, glanced at him then turned away, her scarf allowing only a glimpse of her cheek. The auto driver was taking the moment to rest, maintaining a watchful eye on the signal.

As the light turned green, the tightly packed vehicles spread out once again until the next light, when the process was repeated. Trucks and cars would take the bulk of the space with auto rickshaws filling smaller spaces, then scooters and motorcycles completely compacted the shivering mass of vehicles. The Rolodex in Dean's mind flipped back to his college biology class. *Interstitial spaces, I think that's what they call it. The scooters are filling the interstitial spaces. It's like this whole place is one breathing, vibrating organism.* Another light turned green, and the traffic repeated its serpentine flow through the city streets, like the cells of a snake loosely tied together. Absence of markings or any respect for lanes bred this organic harmony.

Arriving at Electronic City, Dean marveled once again at the contrast of ultra-modern glass and steel high-rise buildings with corrugated steel huts. *There seems to be a real dichotomy here.* The wide boulevard allowed for greater speed, a mixed blessing as the taxi braked hard and made a quick left turn onto a winding street that appeared to lead to a park. The grassy lawns and trees were a welcome relief, punctuated by occasional low-rise buildings.

"This looks like a quieter part of town," Dean remarked.

"Yeah it is. I'm glad our office isn't in one of the high-rise buildings. This is much nicer," Becky replied. "Oh, here we are. Our office is in that older beige building up ahead. Now don't expect anything like the hotel. We're low budget here."

"Sure looks like it."

As Becky paid the taxi driver, Dean surveyed the landscape. *I wonder what today will bring. I sure hope we can figure out how far along these folks are.*

"All set, let's go."

Dean followed Becky into the lobby as she headed for the brightly dressed receptionist straight ahead.

"Hi, we're with DandaData... Just a minute, I've got my badge somewhere in my purse. Dean, do you have your badge?"

"Sure. Let me dig it out of my briefcase... Here you go," Dean said as he placed his badge in his palm and displayed it to the receptionist.

"Please sign in Mr... Ed-monds." The receptionist flashed a brief smile.

Dean couldn't miss her full lips, perfectly planted on a beautiful round face. Her deep olive skin was a pleasant contrast to her bright blue lace sari. *The women here are beautiful, but it seems that they have a wall surrounding them. I wonder what that's about.* "Thank you," was all he could muster in response.

"I should be legal now," as Becky presented her badge.

"Thank you. Please sign in Miss Green. You can take the elevator to the second floor." She once again flashed a brief smile.

I guess she's got her routine down.

As the elevator doors opened, Becky stepped forward into the brightly lit linoleum hallway. "The conference room is down this hallway. Follow me," she said, glancing back at Dean.

Taking in the full view, once again Dean saw that he could be in almost any building in the world. *Not much different than a lot of places I've been. Interesting how there are many ways in which we're not much different.* Turning into the conference room, Dean spied a man and woman conversing at the table.

"Advay, good to see you again," Becky announced.

"You too," was Advay's hearty reply as he shook her hand.

"Hi, Advay. Good to meet you in person instead of over a video conference machine," Dean declared. Looking across the table, Dean noticed the woman rising was dressed less formally, with bright red pants bunched at the ankles, a long loose cheerful orange top with a fluorescent magenta scarf around her neck, draped down her back. *Now why don't the women back home dress like this? Seems much brighter and cheerful.* Walking around the table to greet Becky and Dean, she extended her hand to Dean, "Hi, I'm Priya. I've been on a few of the video conferences with you. How was your trip?"

"It's been great so far. No real snags, and the hotel is great."

"Oh good. I certainly hope you enjoy your time here in India." Turning to Becky, she once again extended her hand, "It's good to see you again. You seem to have arrived intact as well."

"Yep, so far so good. So, how many of the team members are we going to meet today?"

"I've arranged for about 10 or 12 people to come. We'll talk about the project and the progress we've made. Anil will join us at one point to say hello. He's quite busy and so can only meet with us briefly."

"Will we be in this room the whole time? Should Dean and I get settled here?"

"Yes, that should be fine. We can get everyone now that we know you are here."

"That sounds fine. Thank you very much for arranging this..."

Advay responded carefully, "Dean, we have about 45 people working on the project at the moment. We will have the code for you. I'm sure we will. It's coming soon."

The responses were not adequate for Dean. Unsure of the cultural issues, he hesitated to push harder, but felt he must. Deciding to put his cards on the table, Dean pressed on, "Look Advay, my concern is that we're not getting many questions from your guys. If they're working as they should, we expect questions to arise and issues to address. We're not really getting anything, though. We want to get all of the problems flushed out so that we can work on them sooner rather than at the very end. We've got to get this project ready for a GA on July 23rd. We can't have your team missing the deadlines and putting the program at risk. What can we do?"

"I understand your concern, Dean, and I share it as well. We have our team reviewing your documentation and building modules of code to get it working. It's coming along. It will be here. Don't worry."

"How about we do this, Advay? You have the schedule I've sent you previously, correct?"

"Yes, I have it."

"Good. How about you take that schedule and create a set of deliverables with a maximum of two weeks between each deliverable? Could you do that?"

"Mmm, yes, I think we could do that, Dean. When would you want it?"

"How about tomorrow morning? Let's see, it's about 11:30 now. You can gather the team this afternoon and put it together for us to see at 9:00 in the morning? Becky, what do you think?"

"Uh, sure Dean. I think that sounds reasonable," was her unenthusiastic response.

Looking back at Advay, Dean wanted to assess the emotional response to his request. *I hope I didn't push too hard. I hope he doesn't feel that I've pushed him against a wall, but we've got to make sure their pieces get done.* "Advay, do you think you can do it? I know it may be stretching you, but I'd like to keep working for DandaData, and I'm sure you would, too."

"OK, OK. We'll get it for you by the morning. We meet here again at 9:00. Right?"

"Right. Meanwhile, Becky and I will leave you folks to your work so that we don't get in the way."

"Hmm, OK, Dean. Becky, do you need anyone to go with you and Dean, or do you know your way around the city well enough by now?"

Brightening up, Becky responded, "We'll be fine, thank you. Maybe I'll take him to the Jain Temple in Jayanagar and do a bit of shopping there afterward. We can take a taxi there and then he can get his first auto rickshaw ride to the hotel. You game, Dean?"

"Sure, sounds good to me, Becky. Advay, you sure this is OK with you?"

Advay hesitated and then replied slowly, "Yes, yes, this is probably a good thing for us to do, Dean. We'll get it done. We'll get it done. Just a minute and I'll have a taxi called for you. Do you want air conditioning or no air conditioning?"

The team filed into the conference room in silence. There were few smiles and little chatter. Dean leaned over to Becky, "Mmm, perhaps I was a little too aggressive. I didn't feel that I had much choice, though. What we had wasn't working."

"Yeah, let's hope we can work through this without a lot of fallout."

Advay stood at the front of the room and began. "Thank you everyone for coming. Just to review, yesterday Dean requested that we add milestones to our current schedule, milestones that are not farther than two weeks apart. Thank you to all of you who helped pull this together yesterday afternoon and evening. Dean, we also consulted with some of your people in Ann Arbor this morning to make sure we are meshing with your schedule of tasks. There seems to be a bit of discrepancy regarding the schedules, but we've worked through it as best we could. I just want to make sure—the schedule that you sent us two weeks ago, Dean, is the correct one, is that right?"

Dean swallowed hard and felt a knot in his stomach, "Yes... that's the correct one." *Ugh, I hadn't thought that they might contact the programmers in Ann Arbor directly. Of course the schedules don't mesh.*

As Advay powered the projector to life he continued, "So Dean, here is what we've come up with. This is the high level view..."

"And so that is our plan. Dean, Becky, do you have any more questions? Is this what you were looking for?"

The room was silent. Dean and Becky turned to each other, then Dean slowly turned toward the team members in the room. "Folks, I want to thank all of you for putting so much work into this schedule. This is great. Now let me ask you, do you think you can achieve this?"

Blank looks all around. Silence. Dean snapped his head back toward Advay.

"Dean, I think I can respond for the team. We are very concerned about how difficult it will be to meet the schedule, but we think we can make it. As you know, our team here is geared toward the integration work that we have done with Becky's team in the past. We will have to learn a lot along the way. What you are seeing is the face of concern. We are optimistic, but it will be very difficult."

So we've made some headway. They now realize they might be in trouble making the schedule. Fortunately, we've got that three weeks of buffer with the different schedules. Maybe it's best to just drop the rest of this and move forward. That's what Sol said, just move forward, get into the flow. Yeah, that's what I'll do.

Turning back to the team, Dean rose and began to speak. "Once again I want to thank all of you for the hard work that you've put into this project so far. It will be quite an achievement to roll NU technology out into our next version and I want to thank each and every one of you for your part in making that happen. As you saw when you went through the exercise to make a more detailed schedule, this project has many intricate pieces and will require a lot of hard work and innovation. I know that you folks are up to the task, and I look forward to the day that I can stand here and congratulate you for a job well done.

"I know that many of you will enjoy the challenge of creating new, unique software with NU technology and ask that you work with each other and work with the team in Ann Arbor. We can build this product. You can build this product. We intend to have a stellar product in the marketplace, and I hope you enjoy your role in it. Thanks again."

Once again facing Advay, Dean said, "And thank you Advay for pulling this together. I think it's really going to help move us forward."

Dean closed his pad to signal the end of the meeting and others took the cue. Priya turned to Dean and Becky. "Thank you for coming all the way to India. I'm sure your visit will help the team become more energized."

"I hope so," Becky responded.

Advay was packing up his computer and notebook while Priya grabbed her pad and turned toward the door.

Becky rose and turned to follow. "Hey Priya, can we talk for a few minutes?"

"Sure. Come this way."

Taking the opportunity, Dean began, "Advay, could we chat for a bit? Do you have a little time before lunch?"

Sitting back down, Advay responded, "Sure Dean. What is it?"

"I'm not sure if this is acceptable in your culture, but after lunch could I return and just walk and talk with each of the programmers individually? I just want to say 'Hi', and ask them how it's going. Would that be OK?"

Advay hesitated, a puzzled look on his face. "Why would you want to do that, Dean?"

"I want each and every person to know that I care about them and their contribution to the project. I want to make a connection."

"I see, but it's not typically done in our culture. We prefer to follow the hierarchy. It's my job to talk to them."

"Let me ask you this, then. What if I were Dr. Kalam asking you this question? Then what would the answer be?"

Startled, Advay shot back, "How do you know about Dr. Kalam?"

Smiling, Dean responded, "Well, I was in a bookshop yesterday in Jayanagar and saw a photo of a gentleman with long hair and a huge grin. He just seemed to have a glow about him and so I asked, 'Who is this man?' I was told that it was Dr. Kalam, one of your presidents. I inquired as to why he had his picture and was told that a lot of people respect him, that they feel he really cares about them. I was told that he will frequently respond to e-mails sent to him. So now I ask you, what is the difference between me asking you this question in this moment and if Dr. Kalam himself were here asking you this question?"

"Well, Dean, for starters you're *not* Dr. Kalam."

"You're right on that one, but beyond that. Are you saying that I have no credibility or that my skin is the wrong color?"

Advay jerked back. "Dean, I would never say that your skin is the wrong color. We take pride in respecting everyone in India. Our country is made up of more than 10 ethnic groups and that is one of our strengths. We don't care if someone is Tamil, Sikh, Bengali, or even American. Please don't think that."

"Then why can't I talk to everyone?" Dean pressed.

Advay hesitated and Dean sensed an opening. "Dean, you must understand that our culture in this part of the country is geared more toward doing—action. We don't do a lot of that touchy-feely stuff you folks in the States do. We are uncomfortable with open dialog. That's why you didn't get any response when you asked the team members if they thought they could achieve the plan. We have a hard time saying 'no' here. We want to say 'yes,' we want to please. You are correct in that it often comes back to bite us when we don't make a schedule, though. It is difficult for us, but we are adapting to the more structured Western views. Look at some of the products we have been creating. For example, we have had to adapt and learn that our old view of quality, just 'good enough,' wasn't going to make it. Programs such as the six sigma programs that GE and Motorola have used here have helped us tremendously. You mention Dr. Kalam. He is a scientist and helped us become a nuclear power. We didn't achieve that without a lot of thought and care toward innovation and quality. We are making progress, but it takes time."

Wow, I sure stepped on a hot button with that one. He's clearly sensitive there.

"OK Advay, I think I understand better. Thank you for sharing more of your culture. But I'd still like to visit each programmer.

Can we make that happen?"

Advay leaned back, drew a breath and looked up. "OK Dean... you can do it. I have to admit, I'm uncomfortable with it... but you can do it."

Not giving Advay a chance to change his mind, Dean jumped in, "Thank you, Advay, thanks. So when do most of the guys take a lunch break? I can come back when they've settled in after lunch."

"Tell you what. Let's you, me, Priya, and Becky all go to lunch. Then we'll come back around 2:00, and you can make your rounds then. How does that sound?"

"Sounds delightful to me. Thanks a lot."

3... 2... G... Dean took a deep breath as the elevator doors opened, and he stepped into the bustle of the hotel lobby. A new flower arrangement stood at attention in the center of the clerk's circular counter. He surveyed the crowd. *Nothing unusual here tonight. Businessmen in their standard issue dark suits. Smartly dressed women clutching bulging shopping bags. If it weren't for the few women wearing saris, this lobby could appear anywhere in the world.*

His panoramic gaze caught the sign, *Mayura Lounge,* and headed for the doorway, unaware of what was to greet him as he passed through the portal. Squinting in the dimly lit bar, Dean took in the surroundings. Low overstuffed sofas appeared to support the abstract Indian artwork on the walls. Tall bar tables and stools stood like sentinels along the side wall.

A motion caught Dean's attention; it was Becky waving. Brightening, Dean strode toward the bar, details of her curvaceous form becoming evident.

A drink already at her post, Becky stirred and looked directly at Dean. "Glad you could make it. You OK?"

"Yeah. Working with the team here wears on me, though. I did enjoy chatting with each of the team members. I hope it helps. Randy called as I was changing. He was eager to get a progress report." Dean slid onto the neighboring stool. Unsure whether to face Becky or the bar, he chose a compromise as he rested an arm on the bar and angled his seat toward Becky. Glancing at Becky, he didn't want her to know how tempting she was in more relaxed attire. Her tight black halter top dress clung to the curves of her body. "You enjoying being in the hot seat with us?"

"Oh, it's nothing new for me. Since my team is always working on customer integrations we're usually under a lot of pressure to get the project finished so we can get paid. I just wish I got the respect that you development guys get."

Looking up, Dean realized the bartender was patiently standing behind the counter. "May I get you a drink, sir?"

"Sure. What kind of red wine do you have?"

"We have a Merlot and a Cabernet, sir."

"I'd like a glass of the Cabernet, please."

"No problem. It's coming right now."

Turning back to Becky, Dean asked, "What do you mean?"

"You know how it seems that you development guys get all the glory because you're making all the sexy new software. I think they view us integration folks as being off in the backwaters of the big pond. I want to get into the development side so that I can move up." Resting her hand gently on Dean's arm, she added, "Maybe you can help me. I hope that you think I'm doing a good job on this project and can mention that to Randy."

Fortunately the wine arrived so that Dean could break his gaze with Becky. "Here you are sir. My name is Sunil if you need anything else."

Anxious about where this conversation was heading, Dean sipped the wine to buy time. Figuring that a professional approach was a good neutral path, Dean replied, "Becky, it seems that you always do a great job. I certainly have no problem giving you a good recommendation to Randy."

"Thanks, I appreciate that a lot." Becky fondled a button on Dean's shirt and continued, "You know this is our last night in India..."

"Uh, yeah." *Sheesh, how do I get myself out of this one...*

Patting Dean's arm, Becky leaned back and flashed her bright blue eyes straight at Dean. Sipping her own drink, she asked, "How are you liking India?"

"So far I think it's great." He relaxed when Becky backed away. "Fortunately I've not gotten sick, and the people are very friendly and helpful. It is a bit frustrating having to work so hard to keep the project in motion, but I guess if they didn't need us we'd be out of a job, right? How about you? You seem to be enjoying it."

"Yeah, I enjoy it a lot here. It's a nice getaway where no one knows who I am or what I'm doing. Hey, how about if we just eat here at the hotel tonight? I can't really go out like this, at least not to most Indian restaurants. We can just relax here tonight..."

"Uh, sure... sounds good to me. You ready now?"

"So Dean, as you can see we're making good progress on all of the communication modules," Gary stated. "We've clearly got some challenges ahead of us on the interface modules, but I don't think it's anything we can't overcome. The new schedules you and Becky got from the Bengaluru team help as well. They really have become engaged. I don't know what you guys did over there, but you seem to have lit a fire under them."

"Looks great. Maybe we've finally turned the corner on this. Excuse me just a sec folks, let me see who this is," Dean said as he struggled to remove his phone from his pants pocket. "Hello?"

"Dean, this is Randy."

"Hey Randy."

"Dean, I really need to talk to you about something right away. Can you come down to your office?"

"Uh, sure. I'll be down in a few minutes."

"Thanks a lot." Click. *Hmm, that doesn't sound good. I hope I'm not in some kind of trouble.* Dean felt a knot growing in his stomach.

"Listen guys, that was Randy and he wants me to meet with him. It seemed pretty urgent so I better go."

"No problem, Dean. I think we were pretty well wrapped up anyway."

"Yeah, I think so, too. Look, you guys finish the meeting if you think there's more you need to cover amongst yourselves. Sarah, we're meeting at three to go over your update on the work with the Bengaluru team, right?" Dean asked as he closed his computer, grabbed his papers, and rose. He once again sensed that knot in his stomach, as if a soccer ball had taken up residence. A heaviness pulled his body toward the earth.

"Yep, see you then!" Sarah responded.

"Thanks everyone. I look forward to more progress at next week's staff meeting. Thanks again." *Ugh, how can I get out of this job? I can't wait for this to be over. Why does he need to meet so urgently? I wonder if Tony has anything to do with this.*

Rounding the last corner to his office, Dean saw the security guard standing outside his office. Fear struck. *Maybe I should just walk out to my car and be done with it. But I don't have my car keys on me. I guess that decides that.* Continuing down the hallway, albeit at a slower pace, Dean nodded to the security guard and popped his head into his office, hesitant to enter. Randy was sitting at the table, a kraft storage box at his feet. *Now I'm really not liking this. My God, what is going on here?*

"Close the door, Dean," Randy ordered without standing. His arm immediately began trembling. He spoke with a heavy voice. "Dean, remember last week when we talked about the issue that Tony raised, that he said you lied to Advay about the project schedules?"

"Yes, I remember. And I explained that what Tony was saying was not true. We agreed on which schedules to give Advay."

"We talked to Becky about it, too, since she interfaces with the Bengaluru team so much. Unfortunately she corroborated Tony's story, Dean. This is a major problem. You know what it says in our vision and employee handbook, 'Ethical in all our business dealings?' It's a zero-tolerance policy; we've got high standards here."

"Yes," was all Dean could muster through his taut body.

"Well, this is a pretty major offense, Dean. I talked to HR about it first thing this morning. Unfortunately we're going to have to let you go."

"But, but, I don't understand. Don't I get a chance to rebut this? Tony and Becky are the ones lying, not me!" Dean's voice became tighter and louder. "Don't you see that? Tony's been after my team ever since the BenSoft announcement. I'm sure you know that. Can't you see what's going on?"

"Dean, I know that Tony is quite ambitious, but I'm going to have to side with him and Becky on this one. It's a tough decision, and I know it's hard on all of us. Your team will really miss you. You were really hitting your stride, Dean. I'm sorry to see this happen."

"I just don't get it. I've been forthright in all of my dealings with everyone both inside and outside the company. Why does my career here have to end this way? Can't I at least say good-bye to my team?" Dean pleaded.

"I'm afraid not. We need to make a clean break." Kicking the box toward Dean, he said, "I brought this box for you to take some of your personal possessions home right now. We'll make arrangements for you to get anything else that won't fit in the box. We're giving you two months severance pay, and you'll get your final check in the mail. Do you have any other questions before I go? The security guard will escort you to the door. Oh, and I'll need your badge and office door key."

I can't believe this is happening. Surely this is a dream. Tony, that son of a bitch. Looks like he'll finally get my team after all. And Becky was in on it, too. Probably revenge for me spurning her advances in Bengaluru. Damn! Suddenly realizing there was silence, Dean uttered, "Uh, what did you say?"

"I said that the security guard will let you out, and I'll need your badge and office door key. I'm really sorry about this Dean."

Barely able to move, Dean unclipped his badge from the upper lip of his trousers and flung it onto the table in front of Randy. "There." Fighting back tears and struggling to keep his head clear,

Dean grabbed his keys off his desk and unwound the office door key from his keychain. "And there," he said as he flung it across the table.

Numb, Dean quickly looked around but he had no clear thoughts. Only a thick fog. As if on autopilot, he grabbed the few knickknacks on his desk and carefully placed them into the box. *Maybe I should drag this out to make Randy suffer through it. I'm sure he doesn't feel good, either.* Picking up the photo of Jamie, he wondered how he would tell her. *I've been unceremoniously dumped. Maybe that's what I'll say.*

Dean turned back to Randy, "That's all I need. I guess I'm done." *God, I could just sit here and cry. I still can't believe this is happening. A palace coup. That's what it's like. A palace coup. Son of a bitch!*

Randy pressed his hands against the arms of the chair and thrust his hulking body forward. "Good luck to you, Dean. I wish you the best," he said as he shoved his hand out. Dean hesitated. *If I shake his hand it's like sealing a pact. Sealing my fate. Well, I don't have to accept it. Shaking his goddamn hand is like saying, "I accept what you're doing to me." Well no, I don't. Damn you!*

"Goodbye Randy. I still can't believe you're doing this to me."

"I don't have anything more to say, Dean. I'm just really sorry that your career with this company had to end this way." Squeezing between Dean and the wall, Randy clasped the door knob and turned back to Dean, "I'm sure you'll land on your feet, Dean. Good luck to you." And he was gone, the door left ajar.

Standing frozen in his office, Dean hesitated but then realized he didn't want to talk to anyone in his "limbo-land" status. People employed by DandaData were certainly allowed in the building, but those not employed by DandaData were not allowed in the building. So here he was, not employed by DandaData, yet still in the employed territory. *I've really got to get out of here, and quickly, without meeting anyone.*

Dean flipped the lid onto the top of the box, poked his fingers through the holes on each end and hoisted it up against his chest. *Great, now I look just like every one of those guys I've seen walking out of buildings with their little ditty box. There's no dignity. What a load of crap. I may as well be a criminal doing a "perp walk." I've got to get out of here. Geez, maybe I'll run into Tony on the way out. He'd love this sight, wouldn't he.*

Taking one last look around his office, Dean turned toward the door and stuck his head out. Turning to the guard to his left he said, "Let's go," then made a right turn down the hallway toward the side door. The keys jangling on the guard's belt seemed even more ominous than usual. *I really don't want to meet anyone. Pray that I don't meet anyone before I get to the door. Glad my office is on the first floor.* Five more steps and Dean turned to press his butt against the panic bar. Looking up, he glanced at the guard, said "Thanks," and rolled out into the sunshine.

"Good luck to you," he responded, but Dean didn't even look back.

Looking toward the parking lot, he wondered if anyone else was around. *Good, no one in sight. Maybe I can make it to my car unscathed.* As he marched down the sidewalk, the weight seemed to lift from his body. He suddenly felt light, free, and open. *Hey, I don't have to worry about getting this project done now!* The sunlight felt warm against his body. *The birds are singing. I don't remember the last time I noticed them. The sky is a beautiful shade of blue. Wow, maybe there's something else here... I do feel a bit free, but what the hell am I going to tell Jamie? Oh*

God, what a mess.

Reaching his car, Dean balanced the box on one thigh and dug for his keys. He popped open the trunk, dropped the box onto the trunk floor and gently closed the lid. Hesitating, he allowed his last moment in the parking lot to settle in, and then slowly paced to the car door. Seeing himself in the car window, he affirmed that indeed, this was he, and it really wasn't a dream.

Startled from his inner thoughts, he heard a voice and shoes scuffing on the pavement. Looking up, Dean saw a figure trotting toward him, arm raised, "Dean, Dean, hold on a minute."

chapter seven

*We will never discover what lies around
the next corner if we stop moving.*

Wondering what further indignity he was about to experience, Dean maintained his ground. He began to recognize the
stocky form.

"Dean, I'm really sorry, but a dreadful mistake has been
made," she shouted, buying time until she could get to Dean's car.
Arriving out of breath, Tammy stood upright and took a deep
breath. "I don't know if you remember me, I'm Tammy Zeelander,
Vice President of HR. Will you come in and talk with me? You
were right, we should have listened to you. We found out just a
little while ago that Tony is under investigation by the SEC for
shorting DandaData stock just before the BenSoft announcement.
He got a tip on the announcement from his cousin who works
at BenSoft and made a nice bundle of money on the short sale. I

was just going over the investigation with him and he admitted to it, but then he also said he needed to get something else off his chest: the issue he made up about you lying to some guy in India. Listen, will you come back with me right now and see if we can figure out some way to work out this mess? I really am sorry this happened. It's really embarrassing, but let's see what we can figure out."

Dean's body now directly facing Tammy, he just stared at her. *Maybe this really is a dream. Seems like a movie. Her yellow blouse and blonde hair are blowing in the wind just like in a movie. Is this story for real? I don't understand all of this... What about my team? What will they think? I wonder if Jim knows what the hell is going on inside his company. This is so surreal, but, what the hell? I've really got nothing to lose. Besides, Tammy's office is on the other side of the building from mine.*

After what seemed to be several minutes, the words slowly spilled from his mouth. "I'll come. Seems like a lot of people are sorry today, though." His gaze returned to his car, then back toward Tammy, and he began to put one foot forward. Time seemed to have slowed down, but as he took a few more steps the world began to regain its familiarity. He wanted to ask a question but wasn't sure what to ask.

Tammy charged for the far side of the building without another word while Dean straggled behind. *If I come back how would I explain this to my team? How would Randy explain it? I just don't know about this. Maybe Randy's right, maybe we need to make a clean break.* They reached the door and Tammy badged in. As Dean entered the hallway, he looked around and felt a different experience than he had ever felt there before. He was more detached and able to view the place from a distance. He felt he shouldn't be there. He'd just been fired.

They entered Tammy's office and he closed the door. Tammy flopped into her desk chair, and once again gasped for a full breath of air. "Listen, Dean, I've told you the background, now we've got to figure out what to do next. First let me ask you, I know this has been traumatic for you, do you even want to come back? Clearly we've treated you harshly and unfairly, but what are your thoughts or do you need some time to think about it?"

Dean hesitated to collect his thoughts, which was difficult since it seemed as if his head was still spinning. Glancing around at Tammy's office, all he could really see was brown, mahogany brown. Any details were imperceptible to him. *If I immediately say I just want out, then that would be closing the door for good. Maybe I should buy some time.* The words once again emerged slowly. "I think you're right, Tammy. I need some time to think about this. Can you give me a day or two?"

"Sure, it's the least we can do, Dean." Thrusting her card toward him, she said, "How 'bout giving me a call tomorrow afternoon and letting me know what you're thinking then? And how about if we tell your team that you needed to take a break for personal reasons and that you should be back in a few days? Is that OK?"

"Uh, yeah, sure, I guess so. I really need a bit of time to digest all that has happened."

"Sounds good." Rising, Tammy continued, "I'm afraid I'm going to have to run. We've still got Tony to deal with—we've got to figure out what to do for the SEC. I hope you'll stay with us, Dean, but if you don't, I definitely understand."

Dean recalled the last time he sat on the stage watching all of Randy's employees file into the auditorium, when project Phoenix was announced. It was a bit uncomfortable being the only one onstage with Randy, however, especially given the events of the last four days. *I hope these guys take this news well. I wonder what Tony's up to at this moment. I wonder if Becky even came. Hmm, I don't see her out there—oh wait, there she is. She's not looking too happy to see me here. I wonder what kind of rumors have been flying. Amazing how she saved her job by helping out with the investigation of Tony.*

The number of people entering was trailing off and Randy turned to Dean, "Ready to start?"

"Sure, any time you are."

Randy approached the podium and began to speak into the microphone. "I want to thank all of you for coming here this morning on such short notice. I promise you that this will be the shortest meeting that you've ever been to in this auditorium. Dean and I both have a few things to say and then we'll open it up for questions. Now I'm sure that the rumor mill has been chock full these last few days. I've even had a few relayed to me since Monday. Some of the events we can talk about and others we can't."

"For starters, I will confirm to you that Antonio Androni no longer works for DandaData. Unfortunately, for several reasons, I can't go into the details of his departure. Obviously one of the next questions is, Who will fill his spot? I'll get to that in a minute."

"Secondly, I know it's been obvious to you that Dean has been missing from our midst since late Monday morning. It was as if he disappeared, and indeed, he did. We had a misunderstanding on a personnel issue at that time and Dean, myself, and some folks in HR needed time to review and discuss what was going on and determine the best plan forward for all of us—including Dean's team and everyone else he worked with."

"And so, I'm happy to report to you that Dean is back with us and ready to get back to work."

"Now, for the third and final issue I need to address, who will fill Tony's role. As you well know project Phoenix is crucial to DandaData's survival, and therefore we knew that who to place over the mainline software development was a very important decision. We looked at many different options and many different candidates, but in the end there was really only one viable candidate. I'd like to announce to you that Dean Edmonds will be your new head of Software Development!"

Spontaneous applause erupted and all eyes were on Dean. People began whistling and rose to their feet. Astounded, Dean rose and began clapping himself. A broad smile grew across his face as emotions welled up inside him. *I can't believe this, they must really like me! My goodness, I'm just blown away.* As Dean watched the crowd, his awareness began to recede into his body, and he observed the crowd from a more detached state. He felt his mind and body begin to expand, as if he were an energy permeating the auditorium. *So this must be the flow, the zone, that Sol was talking about. Wow, I like this... I feel as if I'm a wave, wafting out over a sea of faces. I feel perfectly content and at peace in this moment.*

Once again, Randy began to speak and Dean slowly came back to the stage. "But there is one more thing. You all have a large task. While I was in discussion with Jim Sousa regarding the placement of Dean in this role, I reminded him that Tony was a Director level, and that this position truly qualifies as a

Director level position. It took some work, but I was successful in convincing Jim that Dean should be the next Director of Software Development. Congratulations, Dean." Once again Randy's employees burst forth into applause.

As Randy leaned on the podium and turned toward Dean, he flashed the biggest smile Dean had ever seen from him. *Wow, I hadn't expected this little twist.*

Beaming, Dean advanced toward Randy and asked, "Should I wait here for more or is that it?"

Randy chuckled and responded, "No, that's it, Dean. Congratulations again."

"Wow, thank you all. I certainly hadn't expected this welcoming reception! I'm honored to be given this vote of confidence by the upper management of DandaData. I want you to know that I am continually impressed with how diligently all of you have been working to make Phoenix and DandaData a success. You're the ones who are making this happen, not me, not Randy or any of the other management here. We're merely facilitators giving you the environment and direction within which to work. Thank you for all that you have done and will continue to do.

"As most of you know, especially the folks who were on my previous team, we called ourselves Team Alpha as a continual reminder that we want to stay on top. We want to be top dog. I'm pleased to announce that all of you are now Team Alpha! We have a task of creating a fantastic new piece of software, and we are on track to do it better than our competition.

"I have absolutely no doubt that you will pull this project off and that it will be very successful in the marketplace. I look forward to the day that we can sit across the table from a customer and hear him or her tell us how much their DandaData software has helped their business. Thank you again and I look forward to continuing to work with each and every one of you. Are there any questions?" *Wow, things are looking pretty good... I really need to share this with Sol. He was a big part in it.*

"Good afternoon, I/O Psychology Department, may I help you?"

"Yes, I'm trying to reach Dr. König."

Silence hung on the line.

"...I'm sorry sir... but... Dr. König passed away two weeks ago."

What? Surely I didn't hear that correctly.

"Excuse me, ma'am?" An aching emptiness filled Dean's body.

"He passed away two weeks ago. I guess you weren't informed. I'm sorry..."

"Um, I'm sorry too... May I ask what happened?"

"He had an aneurysm. By the time they got him to the hospital, there was nothing they could do. Of course we all miss him tremendously. He was such a personable man. Are you an acquaintance of his?"

"Yes..." Tears began to well in his eyes. "We spoke occasionally and he was always a huge help... OK... Well... thanks."

Dean slowly placed the handset back in the cradle. Dean had no idea that Sol had been so important to him. He felt a loss as if the air were being sucked out of an airplane at 30,000 feet. *I can't believe he's gone. This has got to be a dream. I felt so connected to him. He can't just disappear. Who can I turn to now? Will I have to do this on my own?* Bringing his consciousness back to the real world, Dean felt that he needed to reach out and touch Sol one more time, somehow. Surely his family is suffering their loss. He picked up the phone again...

"Good afternoon, I/O Psychology Department, may I help you?"

"Yes, this is Dean Edmonds. I just talked to you about Dr. König."

"Yes?"

"I'd like to write a note to his family. Is he survived by a spouse or children? Perhaps I could write to them and tell them how much he meant to me. It may provide them with some comfort."

"Sure, Mr. Edmonds. I'm sure his wife would appreciate a note, and he has two children. Her name is Wilma König. Just a minute, let me find the address... Here it is. She lives at 3125 Greenleaf Boulevard, Ann Arbor, Michigan. The zip code is 48104. It's very kind of you. Is there anything else I can help you with?"

"No, I think this will do. Thanks again." Once more, gently placing the handset back in the cradle, Dean leaned back into his chair, closed his eyes, and allowed his thoughts to wander—and the tears to flow. His elbows on the desk, forehead cradled in his palms, Dean wept, rocking his head from side to side. *I can't believe he's gone... Who can I turn to now? There's no one else I know who has the knowledge and experience he has. He really was a special person. He could create a rapport with anyone, and they would feel a deep connection to him—if they allowed themselves to have that connection. I wonder how he did that. Oh, I wish I'd taken the time or had the opportunity to ask him. I wonder if I could ever get a rapport like that with my team members. I guess it's up to me now. Sol, wherever you are, if you're even anywhere, thanks. The world will truly miss you.*

There's still one more loose end to clean up... How can Becky and I work together after she did that to me? I wonder how Sol would have handled this. Hmm, I'll bet he would have used the direct approach, just sat down with her. Oh God, I really don't want to do that, though. That is so painful. Mmm, but it'll also be painful seeing her in the hallway and in meetings. Maybe I can just talk to her right now and get it over....

Good, her door is open. Dean knocked lightly and peered in.

Startled, Becky jumped, rattling the papers in her hands. Looking up and seeing that it was Dean, her body shrank into the chair. "Uh, oh, I'm sorry. You startled me." Her voice turned icy. "What can I do for you, Dean?"

"Becky, can we talk? I'd like for us to put some of the past behind us."

"Uh, sure. Have a seat."

Dean closed the door and sat, wanting to appear as open as possible because he did not want Becky to become defensive. "Look, Becky," he said as his voice began to crack. "This is really hard for me to talk about, but I would like for us to continue to work together, and in order to do that I think we need to talk. Otherwise you and I will continue to have this elephant in the room with us."

"Yeah?" She turned her head slightly away, wary of his true intentions.

"First, I want to say that I'm not angry about the story you told Randy regarding the schedules, but I do need to understand why you did it."

"But Dean, isn't it obvious to you that if Tony and I were rid of you I could likely get more people and move into a development role while he could pick up your team?"

"That's what I figured, but I didn't want to assume anything. So that's it? Just that?"

Becky hesitated, placed her hands in her lap, looked down at her dress, thought for what seemed minutes to Dean, and then continued slowly. "Well, there is more." Looking up her faced softened. "Dean, I have to say that I was angry when you rejected me in Bengaluru. It really hurt me deep inside. I felt unattractive, undesired. I guess I wanted to get back at you for that. And now I feel ashamed that I tried such a thing, really both things. I really feel that I can't face you, Dean. I don't feel good about it at all."

Silence crept in and Dean allowed the statements to drift into his core. He felt a sadness, a heaviness that despite doing what he knew as right, he had hurt her. Summoning the energy to speak and clamoring to move beyond the emotion, he slowly responded, "So, let me make sure I understand you... You feel bad that you tried to get rid of me and that you tried to seduce me, and also, you felt bad at one point because I rejected you... Is that correct?"

Becky hesitated, then replied, "Yeah... I think that pretty well sums it up."

"Is there more?"

"No... I don't think so." Hesitating, then continuing, she said "Listen, Dean... I'm really sorry I put you through all of this. I've already talked to Randy about taking a different job in the company. I don't think I can work like this."

"Do you mind if I talk for a moment?"

"Sure, go ahead..."

"First off, Becky, I understand the issue with Tony, and I can live with it. I understand why you did what you did, and I can forgive you for it. I don't condone it and still disagree with it, but

I can live with it. Your words and your body language indicate to me that you do seem remorseful about this, and I appreciate that. I hope that it's for real. As for what happened in Bengaluru, I don't fault you for that Becky. There are probably many reasons for what you did. And just for the record, I didn't reject you because I find you unattractive—quite the contrary. But, you and I both have spouses we need to honor, and I didn't—and don't—want anything to get in the way of my relationship with Jamie. You have your relationship with your husband and it's none of my business what type of arrangement that is, but for me I want to stay true to what Jamie and I have stated our relationship will be. So it's not about you, it's about me. And once again, Becky, I don't fault you for what you did. Does that make sense?"

Looking down again, Becky fidgeted with the folds of her dress. "Yeah... it does."

Dean saw a tear begin to emerge from the corner of her eye but remained silent.

"Oh Dean, I really am sorry. Sometimes I just get too wrapped up in this striving to achieve and then do stupid things." Looking directly into Dean's eyes, "I'm really sorry."

The tears were now welling large in her eyes, and Dean wasn't sure what to say.

"Becky, you don't need to give me an answer now, you can take some time to think about it, but I would like for you to stay and help finish Project Phoenix."

Reaching behind for a tissue, Becky dabbed at her mascara and blew her nose. "If you think it'll work, I'm willing to give it a try, Dean." Blowing her nose once more, she continued, "Thanks for coming to talk to me, Dean. It was certainly easier to run away, but I have to admit, I feel better having talked about it. Yeah, I'd like to try to stay. Thanks."

"Let's go ahead and get started. I'd like to welcome everyone to the first staff meeting with our fully integrated team. I know that it's going to be a bit unwieldy as we've gone from five team leaders in the meeting to 14. I've extended the time of our meetings from 9:00 to 10:00 to 9:00 to 11:30. It means that we'll all have to be very intentional about being brief in these meetings, and we'll probably have to take more issues offline for further discussion. And, I'm open to changing how we run the staff meetings or even reconfiguring how we communicate within our group if necessary.

"For you folks who are coming under me as your manager, I realize that I've not yet had an opportunity to get around to speaking with you individually, but I will be doing so in the next two weeks. So, to start off, I want to make sure that everyone knows what the other teams are doing, so let's go around the room. Introduce yourself and your team's activities. Phil, you're right next to me, so let's start with you..."

"Thanks a lot for the introductions. I think that will get us off to a good start. My second task today is to make sure that everyone is on the same page regarding our work values, priorities, and leadership process. This is a topic that I'm very passionate about and feel is very important for every organization. So let me bring up the first slide. Here you can see the pertinent people and groups regarding leadership, as well as the leadership elements I feel are important.

"The most important is continually focusing on the vision

and goals of Project Phoenix. My philosophy is that if we keep this focus in the forefront a lot of difficulties will fall away. For example, when you have a problem where a team member is wanting to add a specific feature that is not on the requirements list, or does not make progress toward our goals, you can simply ask the question, 'How does that feature get us closer to our goal?'"

Dean looked around the room to observe the body language of the incoming team leaders. *Hmmm, a couple looking down. I wonder if they're the guilty ones...* "It also changes the discussion from a personal one to a more objective one.

"Secondly, in order to have a high performing team you must do a good job selecting and building your team. I realize that we don't have much leeway in that regard at the moment because all of the teams are in place and there will likely be little movement of individuals until the project starts winding down.

"Third, how you motivate your team members is important. We know that challenging work assignments and promotions are good motivators. Next, we need to ensure our activities are in alignment with our superiors, the rest of our organization, and the marketplace. Again, we can look at the examples of the features we're putting in, our schedules, and so forth." Panning the room once again, Dean saw little body language. *I hope I'm getting through to these guys on this...*

"And finally, we must ensure high job satisfaction so that we don't lose the good employees that we have. As I said, for those of you not familiar with this model we'll be discussing it in detail as we have our one-on-one sessions. Today I mainly wanted to give you an overview of the model I like to use so that we have a common language and paradigm within which to work. Any questions?"

A hand rose about halfway down the table. The hand was connected to Frank, a bearish programmer with a short beard. "Dean, I don't get it. What's the big deal here? We're the team leads, and between us and you, and maybe Randy, we're the guys who understand our product best and we know what to do. We just tell the folks on our teams what to do and they'll get it done. Why make it so complicated? Tony always said that leadership was simple—just tell your folks what needs to be done and follow up to make sure it's done."

Needing time to think, Dean looked down and paused. When he raised his head, as expected, all eyes were upon him, wondering how he would respond to this quiz. "Frank, that's a good question. First let me ask you a question in return. Do you enjoy having some autonomy in your job? Do you get more enjoyment out of your job if you make decisions about your work?"

Frank shrugged his shoulder, nodded his head and replied, "Yeah, I guess so. Why?"

"Are your team members really any different from you? Do you think they would like to make some decisions about their work?"

"Maybe. But they're just programmers. I'm the team leader."

Hmmm, this is not going anywhere. Looks like I'll need to handle this one-on-one. "I see. Frank, it seems that this may be a bit longer discussion. Maybe we should take this discussion offline. Is that OK?"

"Uh, sure. Thanks."

"Anyone else?"

An arm inched upward. "Yes, Anton?"

"For you new guys, I just want to say that I didn't really understand Dean's leadership model at first, either, or even see the need for it. But I will say, for the few times that I've had to work through personnel issues with my guys it really has helped. For example, this idea of focusing on the goals has really been tremendous. As Dean says, I was once able to move an issue from a personal issue to a more objective one and was able to diffuse the situation. I hope you guys will take the time to study this and use it."

"Thanks for voicing your thoughts, Anton. Anyone else?" Once again panning the room, Dean saw no reaction. *I hope they get this... and hope they are willing to embrace it and get this code cranked out. I wonder if I can gracefully get these guys to drop those new features they are adding for MozArCo...*

"C'mon in Frank. Sarah and Anton saved that seat between them for you." Dean said, flashing a smile. "Now that you're here we can get started. As I mentioned in the staff meeting yesterday, it's been about two and a half weeks since we've integrated the two groups, and I'd like an update on how well things are flowing, in your opinion, what's working, and what's not. I'd also like to talk about the integration of NU technology into the existing code base.

"Frank, can we start with you?"

"Uh, sure Dean." Frank replied as he leaned back in his chair, his hands clasped together on top of his massive chest. "Things are going pretty well. My guys have been talking with Sarah and Anton's team to get the hooks into the code that they need."

"How has that been going? Are you on schedule?"

Sarah threw one of those 'oh, let's see how he answers this one' looks at Anton.

"Dean, that's kind of hard to say. You see, when we put the schedule together we had in mind a certain order in which the code would come together, but it hasn't played out that way. My guys are looking at it."

"Hmmm, I see. Are they coding anything, or just looking?"

"Oh yeah, they're coding. They've been coding for four months now."

"What exactly are they coding...?"

"Tony had us putting in the remote folder viewing for MozArCo. The code is about 60% complete."

As I thought... "Frank, I know it seems that I'm always asking questions, but let me ask another. Why would you guys be putting that function in when it's not in our goals?"

"I really don't know what your goals are, Dean. Tony just told us to do it and so we did."

Dean wriggled in his chair and leaned toward Frank. "Then I guess we need to do a bit of education. Sounds like a good topic for our next all-employee meeting. But for now, let me make sure all of us are on the same page. The only new function to be in Project Phoenix is to be the NU technology. We may revamp the installation and maintenance interfaces since we need to change them for the NU technology anyway, but that's it." No one moved. "So, Frank, how can we stop this feature you guys are working on and get your team to focus on integrating NU technology?"

"Well, Dean, you're going to have some pretty pissed off programmers if you tell them to yank all of that code out that they've slaved over for the last four months. Plus, as I said, it's about 60% complete. Why don't we just go ahead and finish it?"

This presents a nice dilemma. He has a point... but... "Frank, you know as well as I that any time you put additional function into a software product you risk breaking existing code, memory leaks, in addition to the time and effort it takes to debug the new code. Sarah and Anton, I hate to put you guys on the spot here, but do you have a perspective on this? I know that you've been trying to get the hooks into the existing code base, and it sounds like you've not been too successful."

Anton leaned forward and glanced at Frank. He began to speak, yet began slowly. "I'm really reluctant to take sides here, but Frank, we're really starting to fall behind. What you say is true, that the code modules are coming together in a different order than we originally thought, but it's becoming clear that we're behind, and I'm beginning to think that there is no way we can make the schedule based on what I know now." Anton's eyes shifted between Frank and Dean, hesitant to say another word.

Dean rested his elbow on the table and looked at the floor, shaking his head. Fear crept into his body, bringing that knot to his stomach once again. *I can't face Jim and tell him we're behind schedule... He'll throw me out of that conference room. Shit! Thanks, Tony. Yep, this is Tony's legacy.* He looked up at Frank. "So Frank, what does this mean to you, if the product is behind?"

"I don't see that it's a big deal, so we ship a month or two later. We've done it before. Why should this time be any different?"

Dean felt as if he were about to explode. *Remain calm. Breathe.* He cleared his throat, tensing his body to hold his emotions in check. Dean spoke softly. "Frank... have you looked at our stock price lately?"

"No, why?"

"Because it is painfully obvious to me that you and your team do not understand the urgency with which we must complete this project. Have you been in any of the meetings that Randy has had where he talked about the urgency of the situation?" His emotions began to take over and the energy began to build... "This company is going down the tubes, and you're just sitting in that chair like a bump, telling me, 'Oh, it'll just have to be late.' Meanwhile Sarah and Anton here have their team busting their asses trying to make a July 23rd GA date. This... is... a... big... problem...

"Here's what we're gonna do. First off, Frank, you're going to tell your team *today* to stop coding on this remote folder viewing feature and put them on 100% of their time working with Sarah and Anton's team to get the hooks in for the NU technology. Secondly, I want the three of you to come back here one week from today to show me a schedule that illustrates how you're going to make the July 23rd GA date. Meanwhile, I'll call a meeting with all three of your teams to review the goals of our project and make sure everyone understands the sense of urgency we've got. This company is in serious trouble and everyone—everyone—needs to understand that. Is that clear?"

Dean leaned back in his chair, took a deep breath, and scanned his team leaders. Anton's head was shaking in tentative agreement.

Sarah swallowed hard and spoke, her voice practically a whisper, "Sure, that makes sense Dean. We can do that." She glanced at Frank, looking for a reaction, "And... I think your review with the teams will help us to work together a bit better."

Frank continued to sit motionless and the pause gave Dean a moment to calm down. "I'm sorry I got upset, you guys, but we have got to get this product out on time. Jim has made that abundantly clear... Anything else?" *I can't imagine anyone wanting bring up something else after this little encounter...*

"I don't have anything," Anton replied.

"Me either," Sarah responded.

"Nah, I don't have anything, either," said Frank.

"Let's get going then. Frank, can we chat for a bit longer?"

"Uh, sure."

Sarah forced a half-smile and quickly gathered her papers. Anton rose, emotionless, and both swept out the door, securing it behind them once again.

Dean spoke slowly and deliberately, "Frank, I know there have been a lot of changes here in the last three weeks. How are you feeling about them?"

Finally releasing his hands down to the arms of the chair, Frank relaxed a bit, appearing more open. "Well, Dean, I enjoy my job and enjoy seeing the software products come to completion."

"Good. But how about the changes? You've seen how I run my group, with regular staff meetings and a lot of input from team members and team leaders. Does that sit OK with you?"

"Yeah, it's certainly a lot different from Tony, but, yeah, I can live with it."

"Alright, but, Frank, I'm just not sensing any passion from you. Are you passionate about your job? What fires you up?"

"Hmmm, I never really thought about it, Dean. I really don't know. I guess I'd have to think about it some."

"Please do, because, Frank, I need people on my team who are passionate about what they do. Passionate to create the best product they can—on time. I also need to ask you about your team. When you tell them to stop working on the remote folder viewing feature, what do you think will be their reaction?"

His hands returning to his chest, Frank responded, "My guess is that they're going to be pretty pissed off. They've worked a long time on this feature."

"Hmmm, and what are your thoughts as to how we can manage that problem?"

Frank looked up and then back down at the table. "Well, I don't really know. I'm not sure. I guess we just tell them to stop on the remote folder viewing feature and start working 100% of the time on the NU technology. I guess they'll just have to suck it up."

Dean thought for a moment, drumming his thumb on the table. "How about this... You look at my calendar and set a time for a meeting with your group today or tomorrow and I'll tell them. They have got to understand the urgency we're under and why we're making the change. Is that OK?"

"Sure. No problem."

"Anything else for me, Frank?"

"No, I can't think of anything," he said as he peered down his chest.

"I'll look for a meeting notice, then. Thanks."

"No problem," as Frank slowly extricated his body from the chair.

Wow, I hope I can get this guy engaged. Talk about detached...

"Good morning folks," Dean began. "You're not looking too chipper this morning. I hope you all just had a crummy weekend and that it's not bad news. Let's go ahead and get started. Anton, let's start with you. What's the status of your team?"

"Dean, it's *not* good news. Actually, all of us team leads had several meetings last week... and we've got a problem. We're finally coming to the conclusion that we're not going to be able to hit the July 23rd date. We're supposed to have our full function beta ready on April 23rd, almost exactly two months from now. Based on our coding rate, and our new problem open and close rates, there's no way we're going to be able to make the date. Right now our best estimate is that we're going to be about four weeks behind."

Dean looked down and thought for a moment, that knot in his stomach growing again. "Hmm, are the problems in any one area or any one team?"

"The problem really comes from many different areas and can't be blamed, or pinpointed on any one particular part of the project or particular team."

"OK... I assume there is no one else we can bring in to help, to add more resources?"

"Correct, we looked at that, but the problem is that we're so close to the final code that it wouldn't help to bring any additional folks on."

"So let me see the detail behind this on the project charts. Can you show that to me?"

"Sure." Anton grabbed the stack of papers he had prepared and handed it to Dean. "We thought you might ask for it so we prepared the latest full project detail for you. If you look at..."

Dean just sat in his chair with a blank expression, looking forward but not focused on anything. *I need to think clearly. Oh, I wish there were something we could do about this. Damn.* "This is clearly a major problem, but I guess you're right, we'll have to delay the GA date. I don't know about the announcement date. That's a decision Jim will have to make. Oh, this is not going to be pretty. Jim is not going to take kindly to this. Our next review meeting with him is a week from today. There won't be much forgiveness, I'll tell you that...

"The point I'll need to drive home is how much better we know our product is than BenSoft's. Sarah, the work that your team did to make installation easier and faster is key. Gary, your team's work to improve the user interface is also important. I want to show him that we've been using our time wisely and that when it gets out we feel it will be a superior product, that these improved features will help sell our product over BenSoft's.

"I'll talk to Randy about how we should handle this, but my personal opinion is that we should ask for two months just to make sure. There will definitely be no forgiveness if we have to delay again.

"Let's do this. We clearly can't reset the schedule yet so keep marching to the existing schedule. Look for any way to save a bit of time here and there. We know our orders were to provide the same functionality as the previous product, but we clearly made improvements in areas we had to change anyway. Maybe we could drop some diagnostics that we could pick up in a maintenance release. Tell your guys to look for any places they can save even a day here and there. I'll get on Randy's calendar and talk to him about this and figure out what we're going to tell Jim and recommend to him. Is there anything else I should know?"

"Dean, I just want to say one thing," Gary said. "You mention the new user interface, and, you know, if you hadn't encouraged us to continue to go to our society user conferences and meetings we definitely would not have had the product that we have. I want you to know that I appreciate that, as does my team. What it has allowed us to do is to take the time to create a really stellar product, whereas a company like BenSoft cobbles some technology together and pushes a product out the door. Hopefully we will get more sales as a result, but I know that it has kept my team more viable and renewed, able to always stay on top of the new technologies. So, thank you for your leadership, Dean. Maybe that will help you in your conversation with Jim."

"Thank you for sharing that, Gary. I appreciate the nice thoughts and words. I'll definitely swing back around to you to gather some information for the meeting with Jim. Anyone else?" Pausing and slowly scanning around the room, Dean concluded, "I'll see all of you next week if not before. Gary and Sarah, can you hang around for a few more minutes? I'd like to chat about some charts for my meetings with Randy and Jim. Clearly I want to accentuate the positives of our product." *I just hope it's me who gets to finish the product. So I'm under stress here. Now how did I react? Sol said to observe how I feel, that mindfulness stuff. Hmm, I feel pretty stressed, that's for sure. But do I feel calm about this? Let's see, and how did I react to the news? Calm. I don't want these guys to feel threatened, but I don't want them to feel like they're off the hook and not accountable, either. Yeah, I think I feel about as good as I can about it...*

As Dean marched toward Randy's office his mind began to imagine scenarios. *We could go in to Jim, and he could fire me like the service manager. He could just chew me out and tell me they made a mistake promoting me to this position. I could just quit. Hmm, that wouldn't look good on my résumé, though. Oh God, I really wish I were somewhere else at this moment. Really, almost anywhere else. Well, but here I am...*

Seeing that Randy was intensely typing at his computer, Dean knocked lightly on the door.

Randy looked up. "Hey Dean, c'mon in. Have a seat. From the subject on your meeting notice I couldn't tell if this was going to be a good news meeting or a bad news meeting. Judging from your body language, it's not looking good."

Maintaining eye contact with Randy as he sat, Dean began. "No, it's not, Randy. In a nutshell, it looks like we're running about a month behind schedule. I'll take you through the details I've got, but if you'd like to meet with some of the team leads we can do that as well."

"Hmm... I was afraid of this... Yeah, let's see what you've got..."

Randy's arm was flinching once again, his body crumpled over his desk. "Dean, I really don't want to have to go in to see Jim with this news. He's going to drop kick us out of there. Are you absolutely sure there's no way to make the schedule?"

Dean sighed, hesitated, and then spoke. "Randy, I don't want to have to do that either, but I really don't see any other way. We could wait to tell him when we get closer to our full function date, but I'd rather take the hit now and ask for a two-month delay and get it over with. I know it's not easy, and I certainly fear for my job, but I really don't see that we have much of an alternative. We also definitely need to accentuate the positive features of our product over BenSoft's, too."

Randy looked up and leaned back in his chair. "Oh Dean, this is not going to be pleasant. We can use most of the charts you've got here for our status meeting with Jim. Make some backup charts for some of the detail, though. Can we review them sometime on, say, Thursday?"

"Yeah, sure, I can do that."

"I do want to talk with the team leaders, though. Hopefully if they see me at a meeting they will realize the seriousness of the situation. How often do you have status meetings?"

"Once a week. Every Monday morning, why?"

"I just wondered. I want to make sure you're keeping a good finger on the pulse of the project." Randy sighed. "Oh, I don't like this one bit. What a pain."

"Yeah, it is. I'm sorry about this, Randy. I do want to say that I think the team is really committed to the project, and I commend them for fessing up now before we were right at the full function date, though."

"Well, that is good... OK, Dean. Let's go ahead and set up a time to follow up on this..."

chapter eight

Persistence and willingness to move through
our fear pay great dividends.

Dean eyed the mound of snow at the end of the parking lot as he turned in. The bronze glow from the streetlights cast a pall over what could have been a white glistening heap of snow crystals. *Cold. Yep, I feel pretty cold right now. This is not going to be fun. I hope I have a job after this meeting. I hope I'm not demoted. I hope he doesn't yell at me. There's got to be an easier job somewhere else.*

At the early hour there was no shortage of parking spaces. Dean pulled into a spot just three cars from the entrance. *I feel like I'm going to my own funeral. Maybe I'll hear some funeral processional music as I walk to the conference room.*

Emerging from between his car and the next, Dean heard the ice crunching under the wheels of an approaching vehicle. Looking up, Dean saw Randy's car heading toward him, headlights ablaze. Not eager to get to the meeting, Dean watched as Randy swung into a spot and stopped his engine. His melancholy mood lifted a bit as Randy emerged from his car. *Safety in numbers, I guess. Hmm, maybe this gets back to the herd instinct. As we gather together, we feel we're more likely to fend off our attackers and we individually are less likely to be attacked. Strictly speaking, my chances are now 50:50 instead of 100%. Gee, what pleasant thoughts...*

"Hey, Randy. Morning."

"Good morning to you, Dean. I'm eager to get this over."

"Yeah, me too."

Seeing their breath in the cold morning air made Dean even colder as they walked toward the entrance.

"Look, I'll do most of the talking, and in fact, I'm not even going to hook up my computer. I'd just rather talk about the issues, see if we can get him to agree to the two month slip and then get out of there. Sound good?"

"Yeah, sounds like a decent plan to me. Of course, with Jim you never know what to expect."

"Yeah, I hear ya."

Approaching the entrance, the click of the door lock broke the monotony of the sound of ice crunching under their feet.

"Here we go..." Randy sighed. Dean was speechless, just looking ahead...

"Well, sir," Randy began. "We don't come with good news today. I'll cut to the chase. Right now, based on our coding and testing progress as well as our problem open and close rates, we feel that we're about four weeks behind our schedule. We have a full-function date of April 23rd and right now we don't see a way to make that." Ploughing ahead without hesitation, Randy continued, "On the good news side, we're getting very good reports on our new installation routine with the NU technology and high marks from testers on the new interface for installation. We truly believe we'll have a superior product to BenSoft's."

Having gotten it all out, Randy looked directly at Jim, attempting to gauge his reaction, but there was none. Jim sat silent, staring ahead, turning his pen over and over.

After what seemed like minutes but was in reality seconds, Jim inhaled deeply and began to shake his head. He spoke slowly. "Gentlemen, I just don't know what to say. Do you remember early on when I said that this project cannot fall behind schedule?" Raising his eyebrows, he repeated, "Do you remember that?"

Dean and Randy quickly glanced at each other and nodded in agreement, then looked back at Jim, stiff with fear.

"OK, good... And so now you're telling me that you're behind schedule. What am I to do with this? This isn't supposed to be. Our annual meeting is in four weeks. We keep getting questions on our quarterly calls about when we're going to have a product with NU technology, and all I can say is, we're continuing to look into it and we view it as a direction for the future but we have no product announcement at this time. Blah, blah blah. I can't keep doing this, folks. I... need... a... product. And now you tell me it's going to be a month later that you'll have a product.

"Our stock is now at 35 dollars. Remember when it was 78? I just got our year end numbers last week. Our licensing revenue is down 60%... Down 60%... Fortunately our upgrades, maintenance, consulting and education revenues haven't fallen as swiftly, but they're taking a hit as well. As best we can tell, we've lost six points of market share. This is a disaster, my friends...

"Who do you have working on this project? Dean, why did we ever keep you? Why the hell did we promote you? Are you truly up to the task? C'mon guys..."

The scowl on Jim's face could have vaporized a child. Afraid to speak, Randy and Dean remained silent.

"So you see my perspective... Now, what is your proposal? It seems that *for the moment*, I am at your mercy. I need your product."

Silence hung as Randy and Dean glanced at each other once again.

Randy swallowed and began to respond. "Sir, we clearly do not want to have to slip the schedule again and so we don't want to make it absolutely tight against the current development run rate. So what we'd like, uh, what we're asking for is to declare a GA date, uh, of, uh, September 24th. That would be a, uh, two month slip. We feel that will give us a small margin of error for unforeseeable problems that may crop up."

Jim remained silent, simply shaking his head and biting his lip. He looked down, captured in thought, then slowly raised his head and took a deep breath.

"OK gentlemen. You've got your two months. But let me make one thing clear: if you do not make the September 24 GA date, there will be two other folks in here giving me status reports and finishing the project, is that clear?"

"Uh, yes sir," Randy replied.

"Good. And further, when this project is finished, I want a review, a postmortem. I want to know what worked well and what didn't work well. I want to know what improvements you'll be making to your processes, what new technologies helped and what didn't, and so forth. Got it?"

"Yes, sir."

"Anything else, or do you have any more turds to drop on me?"

Randy and Dean looked at each other, ready to bolt from their seats.

"No, sir," Randy replied.

"OK, good. Although I hesitate to use that word during this meeting. You've not gotten my week off to a good start. You folks get an F-minus today."

"Sorry to be the bearer of bad news, sir," Randy replied.

Jim simply stared at them, and then responded, "See you in two weeks—and I hope you've got better news for me."

"Yes, sir." Dean and Randy rose. Jim remained motionless on the opposite side of the table as he watched them gather their notebooks and computers and quietly exit the room.

As Dean entered the conference room, Gary piped up, "Dean, I saw you in your office, so I figured you dodged the bullet at least somewhat."

"Yeah," Dean replied, still reeling from the meeting with Jim. "It wasn't pleasant, but we survived for a few more months. Let's see, who are we missing? Just Betsy and Frank?"

"They're both at the team leader training session today, Dean. They asked me to report for them and let them know what happened at our meeting—in addition to your meeting with Jim," Anton said.

"Sounds good. Let's go ahead then. First off, as everybody wants to know, yes, I still am employed here for a little while longer. And—we were able to get a two-month delay on the GA date. We've got to work with the marketing and sales folks to reset all of our schedules, pilots, announcement plans, etc. I'll take that one.

"So that's the good news. The bad news is that Jim made it very clear that he will not tolerate another slip in schedule from myself or Randy. So, if you want to continue to have me as your manager, you'll need to get this product delivered on the new schedule. I don't think there's going to be any forgiveness next time. So, when do you guys think you can have a new set of schedules to me?"

Looking around, Anton responded, "I don't know about you other guys, but I think we could have a new schedule by Wednesday."

"How 'bout the rest of you folks?"

"Yeah, I think we can do that," Sarah added.

"I don't see any naysayers, so let's go ahead and set up a meeting for Wednesday. I'll take care of that also. One of the things I want you folks to do is to move the dates to the new schedule, but since you feel that we're about four weeks behind, let's use that number and then put a buffer in the schedule instead of just resetting the schedule to the new dates. That way people won't automatically meet the two-month later deadline. We also need to begin to focus on our pilot tests. Sarah, you're in charge of them. Can we get an update on that next week? Of course you'll need to get with the sales folks to coordinate with the customers we'll be using for the tests. I also want to get the entire project team together to discuss this. I'll have my AA set that up for Friday afternoon. I think it's time everyone hears how serious this situation really is. Sound good?"

"Yeah, I think that sounds like a good plan."

"OK, let's go ahead and go around the room and get your updates. Anton?"

Dean began slowly, "Thanks for coming out this afternoon. I know that all of you would rather be doing something more pleasant on a Friday afternoon, but I felt it was important to gather the entire Team Alpha together to discuss the new schedule and talk about our progress. We'll have time for questions at the end as I understand there are quite a few."

Bringing up the first slide, Dean continued, "I want to set the background for our discussion today, so I'm starting with a chart of our stock price. You can see that we peaked at around $78 a share in April of last year, almost one year ago when BenSoft made their announcement. Since then our share price has slid and is now around $35—less than half of the peak price.

"Why has this happened? The primary reason is because people will buy or sell a stock based on their opinion as to whether or not it will likely go up or down. Investors will think a stock will go up when its future prospects for growth and earnings are good. Based upon the fact that BenSoft has NU technology in their product and that ours does not, the market currently does not view us very favorably. I think we can all understand that.

"So why should we care about this? We should care for several reasons. First, it is a part of our image, a part of our brand. Let's face it, everyone wants to work with a winner. Customers will begin to wonder about us if our stock price has declined considerably. We all know that the purchase of DandaData software is a large ticket price and that ongoing maintenance and service of that software is critical for our customers. We sell mission-critical software.

"Another reason that we care about the stock price is that if the price becomes too low, we become a takeover target. I think we can all imagine a scenario where DandaData is purchased by a competitor who then declares that our product is an end-of-life product with no new development. Sure, they could commit to supporting it for some number of years, but all of us would be gone—without jobs.

"Advancing to the next slide, Dean continued with the bleak outlook. "Here is a graph of our market share. As you can see, we've lost about six points of market share. Keep in mind that each point is worth a little over 250 million dollars in revenue. So six points is a huge number. And finally, this last gloom and doom chart shows our revenue. As you can see, licensing is down about 60%. Our upgrades, maintenance, consulting and education revenues are considerably better than that, but still very negative.

"So that's the gloom and doom portion of our discussion today. I'm not telling you this because I want you to run for the doors. I'm telling you so that you understand where I and the rest of the DandaData management team is coming from.

"Now let's talk about something more cheerful. I want to say that all of you are doing a fantastic job. Let's look at how far we've come. As of a week ago, last Friday, you all completed about 80% of the coding with many of the modules completed. This is a tremendous achievement given the nature of merging a new technology into a legacy code base. And as you can see here, you've found a lot of bugs before they got to the customers. This is good because we want solid, reliable, easy-to-use software. What is not good is that we have bugs at all. We... need...

to... write... code... that doesn't have bugs. Period. And when we look at the productivity metrics we see that you folks are really knocking it out of the park. We're getting tremendous feedback from our testers; they like the product and are finding it easy to use and get up and running.

"But unfortunately, it's not enough... We have talked before how difficult a project this was going to be. And you're finding this out. We originally said that we would have a full function beta on April 23rd. Based on the current coding rate and new problem open and close rates, we don't see any way of making that date. It looks like we're about four weeks behind our original schedule.

"And so, when we had our biweekly status meeting with Jim Sousa on Monday morning and gave him this news, I don't think I need to say that it was rather unpleasant. We asked for a two-month extension in the schedule—and we got it. But it was made quite clear to us that there would be no forgiveness if we go beyond the extended date.

"I know that all of you have been working on new schedules this week, and I thank you for that. So here are the highlights of the new schedule. We're looking at a new GA date of September 24th with a final build date of September 10th. But we've only moved the full function date by the one month you are currently behind."

Raising his voice, Dean continued, "So, this doesn't mean you have an extra two months to finish the project. We're being realistic by adding the one month that we believe it will take to finish—but that's it. I want us to show Jim that we can beat the September 10th date. Given the tremendous amount of work that you folks have already done, I believe that you can do this.

"In closing, I want to highlight some of the real breakthroughs you folks have made. For starters, Anton and Sarah's teams have greatly streamlined the installation process with the NU technology. My understanding is that you've invented a few new techniques that may be granted patents. Secondly, Gary's team has taken the opportunity to improve the user interface. Changes had to be made to adapt to the NU technology and so they took the opportunity to utilize ideas they'd discovered at some of their developers conferences. We fully expect these enhancements to allow our product to leapfrog BenSoft's.

"On a more personal note, while I know many of you by name and have had the pleasure of interacting with you, there are some of you that I have not. And so I want to state for all of you to hear that during this development project I have been truly amazed at how well you have worked together. Sure, there have been some conflicts here and there, but for the most part I have seen, heard, and witnessed a tremendous sharing of problem-solving as well as achievements. Every one of you should feel good about that. You've stayed focused on the goal of getting this product out the door and I commend you for that."

As Dean spoke these words he felt his mind and body expanding out into the room, filling the space, entering the zone. He felt detached, yet his energy permeated the team. Just as he could imagine the Internet, or World Wide Web permeating every computer and device over the planet, he could feel his energy expanding throughout the room and beyond. "As for myself, I feel honored to be working with you and can't imagine a better team to be a part of. Thank you."

Dean looked and felt his way around the room to sense the mood. Silence and not much motion. All eyes were on Dean. *I hope I haven't scared them off...*

"Now I'd like to open it up for questions."

A hand shot up in the second row. "Dean, you mentioned a takeover by BenSoft, and we've had a rumor flying around here for quite a while saying that might be a possibility. Can you comment further on that?"

Dean took a deep breath and began, "I've heard that rumor as well and have been asked many a time if it was true or not. First off, if it were true, I probably wouldn't know about it. Secondly, I can tell you that we would not go down without a fight. We truly believe that the product you folks are developing is a vast improvement over their product. You folks know better than I how cobbled together their code modules are, making installation and maintenance very difficult. I personally feel that you folks have a winning product and we're going to deliver that. That's really all that I have to say about it. Anyone else?"

I wonder how many questions there really are out there. A woman near the back slowly raised her hand, looking from side to side, then at Dean.

"Yes, go ahead," Dean responded.

"Do you foresee any layoffs in the coming months?"

"Good question, Susanne. I can tell you that as far as I know, there are no plans for a layoff. Our cash position is still fairly good and laying people off at this point in our development cycle would be incredibly counterproductive from several angles. I don't see it. Next... Anyone?"

Dean looked around the room twice more, feeling his energy retreating back into his body, but again, there was little movement, little body language to read. "Then I guess this wraps it up. Once again, I feel lucky to be a part of such a tremendous team.

Thanks for all your hard work and have a wonderful weekend."

Muted applause began, and Dean once more wondered if he had missed the mark. *I tried to be open about the situation and encouraging that we can get this done. Looks like we'll see if any bolt for the door or stay and crank this product out...*

Dean was delighted to hear the joking and laughing as he entered the conference room. He hadn't seen a smile on his team leaders' faces in quite a while.

Dean began, "OK, guys, let's get rolling. We were supposed to start three of the pilots last week, and I'm anxious to hear how they're going. Sarah, the meeting is all yours..."

"Thanks Dean. Yeah, as you can tell, we're all in a pretty good mood. We did get all three of the pilots started. The other two are still pending, and we're working to get them started this week or next. Each of the installs went well, and we got feedback on two of them already. The third said they're going over their notes and will have something for us in the next couple of days.

"The good news is that the first install went very well; it took only about 11 hours to get it into their sandbox environment, so that was nice. They were very happy with how smoothly it went and really had good comments on the user interface—Gary."

Everyone chuckled and looked at Gary. "Woohoo!" he exclaimed as he thrust his arms straight into the air. *Ahh, some levity for a change.*

"The second install took almost two full days, which is closer to what we expect most users to have. Of course we need to keep in mind that it almost always takes less time to install in a sandbox environment than in production. So, let's keep our fingers crossed, but so far it looks great. We do have some little things to work on, but for the most part it's looking very good, and we may turn these tests over to our field team sooner than we had expected."

Spontaneous applause erupted—a first for a staff meeting! *Awesome! Boy does this feel good.*

Sitar music blared over the audio system. A monstrous banner hung from the lighting alcove, balloons adorned the chairs. Team Alpha members filed into the auditorium, many doing a double take as they saw moving people projected onto the large screen hung on the stage. Watching, they could see members of the Bengaluru team. The India team seemed ebullient as well, despite the fact that it was 7:30 p.m. their time.

Dean, Randy, Jacques Foucault, Jim Sousa, and Anton milled about the stage. Dean approached the podium, looked around the auditorium and back at the large screen. The din continued.

"Everyone, please find a seat if you haven't already," Dean began. He paused for a few moments to allow quiet to begin. "I know that we've been on a long journey, and today is a very important day. It's a day for you to be proud of your accomplishments. Let's travel back in time for a moment. Over two years ago we had a small team working on NU technology and then on April 17th of last year BenSoft announced NU technology in their product. The race was on.

"We began our planning, built our team, even including some of the folks in India. It wasn't easy to create this product we are announcing today. But thanks to your creativity and hard work, we have done that. Before I say any more I'd like to turn the podium over to our CEO, Jim Sousa. After Jim speaks we'll hear from Jacques Foucault, head of Sales and Marketing. Then we'll have a few words from a couple of our team leaders who would like to share some of the more interesting stories from the project, and then I will wrap up with some closing comments. So thanks again for all of your hard work and new creations. And now, Jim Sousa."

Glancing back, Dean saw Jim standing, clapping, and giving the thumbs up, a rare smile on his face. Seeing the broad grin and hearing the applause touched Dean emotionally. *That's the only thanks I need. We've been through a lot. I've been fired, hired, promoted. Team Alpha has come through for us. Wow, to think back to last April. We've all come a long way. I sure have learned a lot. Too bad Sol couldn't be here in body. This is certainly a tribute to him as well.*

Jim walked to the podium, maintaining eye contact with the team while doing so. He hesitated at the microphone. As Dean stared at Jim his awareness seemed to expand, to open. The energy field of his body felt as if he were growing. A silence and stillness entered the space. *Wow, I guess Sol is here... I can feel the flow, I'm in the zone...*

Jim began, "The very first thing I want to say to you folks is, congratulations, and thanks Team Alpha. As Dean said, you've done a tremendous job. Dean talked about the BenSoft announcement last year. I remember it well, too. My heart sank the moment I was told about it. That afternoon and evening I read everything I could about it, and the next day Dean came to tell me what he knew.

"Every two weeks I continued to get progress reports. As Dean could relay to you—but I hope that he doesn't—those meetings weren't always pleasant. It seemed that I was continually told that he and you needed time to do things right. First it was selecting the team leaders, then it was selecting the team members. Then he told me about motivation. I thought I knew all that I needed to know about motivation and didn't want to hear about it. We talked about assuring that you were working toward the agreed upon goals and your vision of the product. He made sure that all of you had the necessary resources and wanted to know that you were challenged and happy in your role on this project. Finally, and most importantly, he ensured that you were focused on creating an outstanding product.

"I have watched Dean develop into an outstanding leader, and I hope you appreciate the role model that he has been. It's almost as if he's had someone whispering in his ear the whole time, providing him with direction.

"I have to admit, there were times that I was skeptical; there were times I was angry. And there were times when I felt I truly didn't understand what you folks were doing. But I had to trust Dean. And I did. That is... until he came in telling me that the project had fallen behind by a month. I can truly say that in that moment I began to waver in my trust.

"But he—and you—have pulled through. You responded to BenSoft's product with a superior one. Sure, they'll catch up to us, but we will then pull ahead once again. And so I want to thank all of you, sincerely, for a job well done. You created an impressive product, using NU technology to its fullest potential, and I know that was not an easy task. Thank you, and again, congratulations for a job well done."

Turning back to face the screen, Jim continued, "For you team members in Bengaluru, you became an integral part of the project, and we certainly appreciate your efforts."

It was Anton's turn at the podium and he approached with caution. "Everyone," he began, his deep voice shaking, "I want to add my congratulations along with everyone else. You have all done a spectacular job. Almost all of you know that I have been involved with NU technology here since we began investigating the possibilities for the technology in our products. It has been a tremendous challenge to complete this project, and I could talk for quite a long time about the technical challenges we've met and overcome. In fact, I was asked to comment briefly about the major technical challenges we've conquered.

His voice becoming more confident, Anton continued, "But that's not what I'm going to talk about... I'm going to talk about leadership, as did Jim, but from a different perspective. As this project was ramping up to high gear, I had my own set of issues I was grappling with. I was frustrated. I was angry. And I told Dean that we needed to talk. And we did talk.

"I got angry with Dean and spewed my drama. And Dean took it. He took it and began to ask me some questions. Very good questions. He didn't push back and tell me to suck it up and get back to work. He didn't tell me that the problems were mine and that I needed to fix them. No. In his own gentle way he asked questions that made me think about what was inside me, about what I wanted to do with my life, about how I felt. After meeting with Dean several times I began to understand this concept of looking inside, finding out who I am."

Looking back at Dean, he continued, "And so, Dean, I want to personally thank you in front of this crowd for helping me to understand myself better and for leading this team to create an awesome product. Knowing how you've touched my life, Dean, I can imagine that you've also touched most of the other lives out here in front of me. So, thank you, Dean. Thank you very much."

His final words were lost, drowned in the applause as everyone rose to their feet. Dean looked out at all the lives he perhaps did touch. He felt his gut moving, and fought back the tears. *I guess I made a few connections...*

Dean rose from his seat and approached Anton, holding back the tears as he extended his right hand and grasped Anton's, clasping his left over the top of the joined hands. He looked Anton directly in the eye, peering into his soul and uttered, "Thanks, Anton. That means a lot to me."

As Anton broke the soulful embrace, Dean turned to the podium and began, "Wow, I can't think of anything to say after that. Just... thanks... thanks a lot..." He surveyed the audience and savored the moment, then continued. "So, does anyone have any questions?"

A hand shot up in the second row. "Yes, Becky."

"Uh, Dean, I sort of hate to ask this, but I got an e-mail from the CTO of MozArCo this morning. Seems that he got an early view of our press release and was asking if his remote folder viewing feature was in this new release."

Oh shit! I can't believe it... Dean's heart sank, his head snapping back to look at Jim and Jacques. "Uh, uh, well, I guess we'll have to think about how to respond to that. Maybe Jacques can help us out..."

A broad grin came across Becky's face and she blurted out, "Just kidding!" The crowd burst into laughter and Dean once again glanced back at Jim and Jacques, who were exchanging puzzled looks. Dean just smiled and let them wonder...

"Hey Dean," the voice crackled over the loudspeakers. "This is Advay. I'd like to add to what Anton said. You know, you pushed us to make a schedule, a detailed schedule, and we didn't want to do it. But in the end it was what we needed. You were right. And some of you people there in Michigan may not know this, but when Dean was here he wanted to talk to each person on the team individually. We don't typically do such things here, and I didn't want him to do it, but I agreed, and I'm glad I did. The team members here really responded to that. They appreciated the individual attention. So, Dean, I also want to thank you for your leadership. You encouraged us to do our best—and I think we did. Thanks."

Amazing... I guess I didn't push too far. "Wow, thank you, Advay! I really appreciate the compliment. Any more questions or comments?" Dean looked over the audience once more. Seeing no more hands, he concluded, "OK, so enjoy the day, and once again, thank you so much for all your hard work."

Randy held his badge to the reader and pulled it away once the green light illuminated and the lock emitted it's characteristic click. "Dean, I hope this is our last review on this project." Heaving the massive glass door aside and holding it for Dean, he continued, "I'm glad the software is finally out and has been so well received. As Jim said, it's a real testament to your leadership, Dean. You've got an impressive team, and they seem to genuinely enjoy working for you."

"Yeah, I guess we have come a long way, Randy. I, too, can remember the day of the BenSoft announcement as if it had happened just yesterday."

Upon entering the CEO enclave, Dean no longer felt the need for a hushed voice or somber tone. Today he was jubilant, excited to have achieved success. Arriving at the conference room, they found both wooden doors sealed and no one in sight.

Randy turned to Dean, "Hmm, I guess they've still got another meeting going on..." Leaning in, Randy said, "Yeah, I hear voices. This is a pleasant switch from the 7:30 a.m. meetings, isn't it?"

Dean nodded and was beginning to speak when a woman approached. "Excuse me, are you here for a meeting with Jim?"

"Yes, we had a 4:30 meeting."

"Oh. He's still in a sales review meeting with Mr. Foucault and a few others. Can I get you folks something to drink?"

"Do you have any water?"

"Sure, I'll be right back with it. Oh, by the way, my name is Amy. I'm Jim's Administrative Assistant. My desk is just behind this wall."

"Thanks," Dean replied. *Sure is a completely different atmosphere when things are going well. Before, we were here so early Amy wasn't even around!* "Randy, I'm not sure if this is good news or bad news that the sales meeting is running late. Any thoughts?"

"I've got to believe it's good news, Dean. All the reports I'm getting back from the field are very positive. We know from the customer meetings we had during the pilot rollouts that our customers viewed our product as superior in capability to the BenSoft product. Now, if we can just translate that into sales we're all—"

Just then one of wooden doors flung open, and people began filing out, some nodding to Dean and Randy as they departed. Still hearing Jim's stern voice, Randy leaned toward the door just enough to see Jim and Jacques still engaged in conversation.

"Listen, Jacques, I really think we've got the product part nailed. Now you've got to get out there and sell the hell out of it. As I said when everyone else was here, it's your job to make sure the message about the superiority of our product gets out there."

"Yes, I understand Jim. You're right, we should be able to do well with this product," Jacques responded.

"If you want to find out more about it, our Development folks are supposed to be in here next. In fact, they may be waiting outside." Rising from his chair and turning toward the door, Jim spied Dean and Randy in the lobby. "Come in fellas, come in."

"Thanks for coming guys. As you're settling in, I just want to tell you that we're continuing to get very good reports from the field. Our existing customers are finding that our product works well in their sandbox environments and pilots, not to mention the few rollouts that we've had. So what do you have for me today? I hope this is the last time we need to meet on this project. Oh, and I hope you've noticed that our stock is up almost ten dollars since the product announcement. Dean, I think we'll be able to help you get a share of that."

"Thank you sir. Thanks a lot," Dean responded.

"We hope this is our last meeting on this project as well, sir," Randy said. "We brought some slides for you, but I would rather just fill you in verbally, if that's OK."

"Works for me. Go on."

"The main thing we want to do is to tie up some loose ends we talked about last time. Does that work for you?"

"Sure, let's go."

"The first item was ..."

"Thanks for filling me in and closing the loop on these items. Jacques, you've been awfully quiet. Do you have any questions?"

"No, I can't really think of any, sir. You guys have done a splendid job. We're getting super feedback from the field. Thank you very much. You clearly knew what you needed to do."

Brightening, Jim looked Dean straight in the eye. "Dean, I want to say one thing. When this flap blew up about that scoundrel Antonio, and Randy came to me wanting to give you Tony's job and position, I was very, very skeptical. As I said at the announcement meeting, I think you've done a marvelous job, and I commend you for it. I'll admit I'm not one of these touchy-feely kind of guys, but it seems that you've really been able to connect with the developers and get them to produce. Thanks."

Caught off guard for a second time by Jim's rare expression of praise, Dean hesitated, but then spoke. "Thank you sir, and thank you Randy, for having faith in me. I certainly appreciate the opportunity to prove myself."

The applause awoke Dean from his reminiscence and worry about his current project. Slowly coming back to the present moment, he knew that he must mentally prepare for his talk.

"Tim, thank you for a very enlightening presentation. Up next we are fortunate to have with us Mr. Dean Edmonds, Director of Software Development at DandaData. Dean has led his team through a major overhaul of their mainstream product. His story is a compelling one of leadership and tenacity. Please join me in welcoming Mr. Dean Edmonds."

Dean rose as the audience graced him with hearty applause.

"Thank you for that kind introduction. First I'd like to set the stage for my talk this afternoon. Get yourself comfortable in your seat. Sit upright, close your eyes and take a deep inhalation... Exhale... Now find yourself in a quiet place. Feel the stillness within you. Now imagine yourself floating down a gentle river..."

REFERENCES

LEADERSHIP RESEARCH HISTORY

Bentz, V. J. (1967). The Sears experience in the investigation, description, and prediction of executive behavior. In F. R. Wickert & D. E. McFarland (Eds.), *Measuring executive effectiveness* (pp. 147-205). New York: Appleton-Century-Crofts.

Bentz, V. J. (1968). The Sears experience in the investigation, description, and prediction of executive behavior. In J. A. Myers (Ed.), *Predicting managerial success* (pp. 59-152). Ann Arbor, Michigan: Foundation for Research on Human Behavior.

Bray, D. W., Campbell, R. J., & Grant, D. L. (1974). *Formative years in business: A long-term AT&T study of managerial lives.* New York: Wiley-Interscience.

Carlyle, T. (1849). *On heroes, hero-worship, and the heroic in history.* Boston: Houghton Mifflin.

Charan, R., Drotter, S. J., & Noel, J. L. (2001). *The leadership pipeline: How to build the leadership-powered company.* San Francisco, CA: Jossey-Bass.

Collins, J. C. (2001). *Good to great: Why some companies make the leap... and others don't.* New York: Collins.

Connelly, M. S., Gilbert, J. A., Zaccaro, S. J., Threlfall, K. V., Marks, M. A., & Mumford, M. D. (2000). Cognitive and temperament predictors of organizational leadership. *The Leadership Quarterly*, 11(1), 65-86.

Craig, D. R., & Charters, W. W. (1925). *Personal leadership in industry*. New York: McGraw-Hill Book Co.

Day, D. V., & Zaccaro, S. J. (2007). Leadership: A critical historical analysis of the influence of leader traits. In L. L. Koppes (Ed.), *Historical perspectives in industrial and organizational psychology* (pp. 383-405). Mahwah, New Jersey: Lawrence Erlbaum Associates.

Fleishman, E. A., Mumford, M. D., Zaccaro, S. J., Levin, K. Y., Korotkin, A. L., & Hein, M. B. (1991). Taxonomic efforts in the description of leader behavior: A synthesis and functional interpretation. *The Leadership Quarterly*, 2(4), 245-287.

Gibb, C. A. (1947). The principles and traits of leadership. *Journal of Abnormal and Social Psychology*, 42, 267-284.

Hogan, R. J., & Kaiser, R. B. (2005). What we know about leadership. *Review of General Psychology*, 9(2), 169-180.

Hogan, R. J., Raskin, R., & Fazzini, D. (1990). The dark side of charisma. In K. E. Clark & M. B. Clark (Eds.), *Measures of Leadership* (pp. 343-354). West Orange, NJ: Leadership Library of America, Inc.

Hollander, E. P., & Julian, J. W. (1969). Contemporary trends in the analysis of leadership processes. *Psychological Bulletin*, 71(5), 387-397.

Howard, A., & Bray, D. W. (1990). Predictions of managerial success over long periods of time: Lessons from the management progress study. In K. E. Clark & M. B. Clark (Eds.), *Measures of leadership* (pp. 113-130). West Orange, NJ: Leadership Library of America, Inc.

Judge, T. A., Bono, J. E., Ilies, R., & Gerhardt, M. W. (2002). Personality and leadership: A qualitative and quantitative review. *Journal of Applied Psychology*, 87(4), 765-780.

Judge, T. A., Colbert, A. E., & Ilies, R. (2004). Intelligence and leadership: A quantitative review and test of theoretical propositions. *Journal of Applied Psychology*, 89(3), 542-552.

Kaiser, R. B., & Craig, S. B. (2004, April). What gets you there won't keep you there: Managerial behaviors related to effectiveness at the bottom, middle, and top. In R. B. Kaiser & S. B. Craig (Chairs), *Filling the pipe I: Studying management development across the hierarchy*. Symposium conducted at the meeting of Society for Industrial and Organizational Psychology Conference 2004, Chicago, IL.

Kenny, D. A., & Zaccaro, S. J. (1983). An estimate of variance due to traits in leadership. *Journal of Applied Psychology*, 68(4), 678-685.

Kets de Vries, M. F. R., & Miller, D. (1984). Neurotic style and organizational pathology. *Strategic Management Journal*, 5(1), 35-55.

Kipnis, D., Schmidt, S., Price, K., & Stitt, C. (1981). Why do I like thee: Is it your performance or my orders? *Journal of Applied Psychology*, 66(3), 324–328.

Kramer, R. M. (2003). The harder they fall. *Harvard Business Review*, 81(10), 58-66.

Lombardo, M. M., Ruderman, M. N., & McCauley, C. D. (1988). Explanations of success and derailment in upper-level management positions. *Journal of Business and Psychology*, 2(3), 199-216.

Lord, R. G., De Vader, C. L., & Alliger, G. M. (1986). A meta-analysis of the relation between personality traits and leadership perceptions: An application of validity generalization procedures. *Journal of Applied Psychology*, 71(3), 402-410.

Luthans, F. (1988). Successful vs. effective real managers. *Academy of Management Executive*, 2(2), 127-132.

Luthans, F., Hodgetts, R. M., & Rosenkrantz, S. A. (1988). *Real managers*. Cambridge, MA: Ballinger.

Luthans, F., Rosenkrantz, S. A., & Hennessey, H. W. (1985). What so successful managers really do? An observation study of managerial activities. *The Journal of Applied Behavioral Science*, 21(3), 255-270.

McCall, M. W., Lombardo, M. M., & Morrison, A. M. (1988). *The lessons of experience*. Lexington, MA: Lexington Books.

Miller, G. A. (1956). The magical number seven, plus or minus two: Some limits on our capacity for processing information. *The Psychological Review*, 63, 81-97.

Mumford, M. D., Zaccaro, S. J., Harding, F. D., Jacobs, T. O., & Fleishman, E. A. (2000). Leadership skills for a changing world: Solving complex social problems. *The Leadership Quarterly*, 11(1), 11-35.

Schmidt, F. L., & Hunter, J. E. (1998). The validity and utility of selection methods in personnel psychology: Practical and theoretical implications of 85 years of research findings. *Psychological Bulletin*, 124(2), 262-274.

Stogdill, R. M. (1948). Personal factors associated with leadership: A survey of the literature. *Journal of Psychology*, 25, 35-71.

Sundstrom, E. D. (1999). Supporting work team effectiveness: Best practices. In E. D. Sundstrom (Ed.), *Supporting work team effectiveness* (pp. 301-342). San Francisco, CA: Jossey-Bass.

Tead, O. (1935). *The art of leadership*. New York: McGraw-Hill.

Zaccaro, S. J. (2007). Trait-based perspectives of leadership. *American Psychologist*, 62(1), 6-16.

Zaccaro, S. J., Gilbert, J. A., Thor, K. K., & Mumford, M. D. (1991). Leadership and social intelligence: Linking social perspectives and behavioral flexibility to leader effectiveness. *The Leadership Quarterly*, 2(4), 317-342.

Zaccaro, S. J., Rittman, A. L., & Marks, M. A. (2001). Team leadership. *The Leadership Quarterly*, 12(4), 451-483.

CREATIVE TEAMS

Allen, T., Katz, R., Grady, J. J., & Slavin, N. (1988). Project team aging and performance: The roles of project and functional managers. *R&D Management*, 18(4), 295-308.

Amabile, T. M. (1985). Motivation and creativity: Effect of motivational orientation on creative writers. *Journal of Personality and Social Psychology*, 48(2), 393-399.

Amabile, T. M. (1997). Motivating creativity in organizations: On doing what you love and loving what you do. *California Management Review*, 40(1), 39-58.

Amabile, T. M. (1998). How to kill creativity. *Harvard Business Review*, 76(5), 76-87.

Csikszentmihalyi, M. (1997). *Creativity: Flow and the psychology of discovery and invention*. New York: HarperCollins.

Csikszentmihalyi, M. (1999). Implications of a systems perspective for the study of creativity. In R. J. Sternberg (Ed.), *Handbook of creativity* (pp. 313-335). Cambridge, UK: Cambridge University Press.

Deci, E. L., & Ryan, R. M. (1985). *Intrinsic motivation and self-determination in human behavior.* New York: Plenum Press.

Feist, G. J. (2004). The evolved fluid specificity of human creative talent. In R. J. Sternberg, E. L. Grigorenko, & J. L. Singer (Eds.), *Creativity: From potential to realization* (pp. 57-82). Washington, DC: American Psychological Association.

Great Place to Work Institute, I. (2008). Great workplaces outperform their peers: Financial results. Retrieved June 11, 2008, from http://www.greatplacetowork.com/great/

Gruber, H. E., & Davis, S. N. (1988). Inching our way up Mount Olympus: The evolving-systems approach to creative thinking. In R. J. Sternberg (Ed.), *The nature of creativity* (pp. 243-270). New York: Cambridge University Press.

Hayes, J. R. (1989). Cognitive processes in creativity. In J. A. Glover, R. R. Ronning, & C. R. Reynolds (Eds.), *Handbook of creativity* (pp. 135-145). New York: Plenum Press.

Jones, B. F. (2005). Age and great invention. *NBER Working Paper No. W11359.*

Katz, R. (2004). Managing creative performance in R&D teams. In R. Katz (Ed.), *The human side of managing technological innovation: A collection of readings* (pp. 161-170). New York: Oxford University Press.

Kaufman, J. C., & Baer, J. (2004). Hawking's haiku, Madonna's math: Why it is hard to be creative in every room of the house. In R. J. Sternberg, E. L. Grigorenko, & J. L. Singer (Eds.), *Creativity: From potential to realization* (pp. 3-19). Washington, DC: American Psychological Association.

Krause, D. E. (2004). Influence-based leadership as a determinant of the inclination to innovate and of innovation-related behaviors: An empirical investigation. *The Leadership Quarterly,*

15(1), 79-102.

Kruglanski, A. W., Friedman, I., & Zeevi, G. (1971). The effects of extrinsic incentive on some qualitative aspects of task performance. *Journal of Personality*, 39(4), 606-617.

Kruglanski, A. W., Stein, C., & Riter, A. (1977). Contingencies of exogenous reward and task performance: On the "minimax" principle in instrumental behavior. *Journal of Applied Social Psychology*, 7(2), 141-148.

LePine, J. A., Colquitt, J. A., & Erez, A. (2000). Adaptability to changing task contexts: Effects of general cognitive ability, conscientiousness, and openness to experience. *Personnel Psychology*, 53(3), 563-593.

Paulus, P. B., & Yang, H. C. (2000). Idea generation in groups: A basis for creativity in organizations. *Organizational Behavior and Human Decision Processes*, 82(1), 76-87.

Pittman, T. S., Emery, J., & Boggiano, A. K. (1982). Intrinsic and extrinsic motivational orientations: Reward-induced changes in preference for complexity. *Journal of Personality and Social Psychology*, 42(5), 789-797.

Probst, T. M., Stewart, S. M., Gruys, M. L., & Tierney, B. W. (2007). Productivity, counterproductivity and creativity: The ups and downs of job insecurity. *Journal of Occupational and Organizational* Psychology, 80(3), 479-497.

Reiter-Palmon, R., Illies, J. J., & Kobe-Cross, L. M. (2009). Conscientiousness is not always a good predictor of performance: The case of creativity. *The International Journal of Creativity and Problem Solving*, 19(2), 27-45.

Rinaldi, S., Cordone, R., & Casagrandi, R. (2000). Instabilities in creative professions: A minimal model. *Nonlinear Dynamics, Psychology, and Life Sciences*, 4(3), 255-273.

Weisberg, R. W. (1999). Creativity and knowledge: A challenge to theories. In R. J. Sternberg (Ed.), *Handbook of creativity* (pp. 226-250). Cambridge, UK: Cambridge University Press.

FIVE-FACTOR MODEL

Barrick, M. R., & Mount, M. K. (1991). The big five personality dimensions and job performance: A meta-analysis. *Personnel Psychology*, 44(1), 1-26.

Briggs, S. R. (1992). Assessing the five-factor model of personality description. *Journal of Personality*, 60(2), 253-293.

Costa, P. T., Jr., & McCrae, R. R. (1992). *NEO PI-R professional manual*. Odessa, FL: Psychological Assessment Resources.

Costa, P. T., Jr., & McCrae, R. R. (1995). Domains and facets: Hierarchical personality assessment using the revised NEO personality inventory. *Journal of Personality Assessment*, 64(1), 21-50.

Digman, J. M. (1990). Personality structure: Emergence of the five-factor model. *Annual Review of Psychology*, 41(1), 417-440.

Furnham, A. (1996). The big five versus the big four: The relationship between the Myers-Briggs Type Indicator (MBTI) and NEO-PI five factor model of personality. *Personality and Individual Differences*, 21(2), 303-307.

Furnham, A., Dissou, G., Sloan, P., & Chamorro-Premuzic, T. (2007). Personality and intelligence in business people: A study of two personality and two intelligence measures. *Journal of Business and Psychology*, 22(1), 99-109.

Goldberg, L. R. (1990). An alternative "description of personality": The big-five factor structure. *Journal of Personality*, 59(6),

1216-1229.

Hogan, R. (2007). *Personality and the fate of organizations.* New York: Lawrence Erlbaum.

Hogan, R. J., Curphy, G. J., & Hogan, J. (1994). What we know about leadership: Effectiveness and personality. *American Psychologist,* 49(6), 493-504.

John, O. P., & Srivastava, S. (1999). The big five trait taxonomy: History, measurement, and theoretical perspectives. In O. P. John, S. Srivastava, & L. A. Pervin (Eds.), *Handbook of personality: Theory and research.* New York: Guilford.

Judge, T. A., & Bono, J. E. (2000). Five-factor model of personality and transformational leadership. *Journal of Applied Psychology,* 85(5), 751-765.

Judge, T. A., Bono, J. E., Ilies, R., & Gerhardt, M. W. (2002). Personality and leadership: A qualitative and quantitative review. *Journal of Applied Psychology,* 87(4), 765-780.

Judge, T. A., & Cable, D. M. (1997). Applicant personality, organizational culture, and organizational attraction. *Personnel Psychology,* 50(2), 359-394.

Judge, T. A., Heller, D., & Mount, M. K. (2002). Five-factor model of personality and job satisfaction: A meta-analysis. *Journal of Applied Psychology,* 87(3), 530-541.

Judge, T. A., Higgins, C. A., Thoresen, C. J., & Barrick, M. R. (1999). The big five personality traits, general mental ability, and career success across the life span. *Personnel Psychology,* 52(3), 621-652.

Judge, T. A., & Ilies, R. (2002). Relationship of personality to performance motivation: A meta-analytic review. *Journal of Applied Psychology,* 87(4), 797-807.

Judge, T. A., Martocchio, J. J., & Thoresen, C. J. (1997). Five-factor model of personality and employee absence. *Journal of Applied Psychology*, 82(5), 745-755.

LePine, J. A., Colquitt, J. A., & Erez, A. (2000). Adaptability to changing task contexts: Effects of general cognitive ability, conscientiousness, and openness to experience. *Personnel Psychology*, 53(3), 563-593.

Lodhi, P. H., Deo, S., & Belhekar, V. M. (2002). The five-factor model of personality: Measurement and correlates in the Indian context. In R. R. McCrae (Ed.), *The five-factor model of personality across cultures* (pp. 227-248). New York: Kluwer Academic/Plenum Publishers.

McCrae, R. R. (1996). Social consequences of experiential openness. *Psychological Bulletin*, 120(3), 323-337.

McCrae, R. R. (Ed.). (2002). *The five-factor model of personality across cultures*. New York: Kluwer Academic/Plenum Publishers.

McCrae, R. R., & Costa, P. T., Jr. (1989). Reinterpreting the Myers-Briggs Type Indicator from the perspective of the five-factor model of personality. *Journal of Personality*, 57(1), 17-40.

McCrae, R. R., & Costa, P. T., Jr. (1997). Personality trait structure as a human universal. *American Psychologist*, 52(5), 509-516.

McCrae, R. R., Costa, P. T., Jr., Lirna, M. P., Simoes, A., Ostendorf, F., Angleitner, A. et al. (1999). Age differences in personality across the adult life span: Parallels in five cultures. *Developmental Psychology*, 35(2), 466-477.

McCrae, R. R., & John, O. P. (1992). An introduction to the five-factor model and its applications. *Journal of Personality*, 60(2), 175-215.

Neuman, G. A., Wagner, S. H., & Christiansen, N. D. (1999). The relationship between work-team personality composition and the job performance of teams. *Group & Organization Manage-*

ment, 24(1), 28.

Piedmont, R. L. (1998). *The revised NEO personality inventory: Clinical and research applications.* New York: Plenum Press.

GOALS

Durham, C. C., Knight, D., & Locke, E. A. (1997). Effects of leader role, team-set goal difficulty, efficacy, and tactics on team effectiveness. *Organizational Behavior and Human Decision Processes*, 72(2), 203-231.

Erez, M., & Zidon, I. (1984). Effect of goal acceptance on the relationship of goal difficulty to performance. *Journal of Applied Psychology*, 69(1), 69-78.

Guzzo, R. A., & Dickson, M. W. (1996). Teams in organizations: Recent research on performance and effectiveness. *Annual Review of Psychology*, 47(1), 307-338.

Kerr, N. L., & Tindale, R. S. (2004). Group performance and decision making. *Annual Review of Psychology*, 55, 623-655.

Latham, G. P., & Seijts, G. H. (1999). The effects of proximal and distal goals on performance on a moderately complex task. *Journal of Organizational Behavior*, 20(4), 421-429.

Likert, R. (1967). *The human organization: Its management and value.* New York: McGraw-Hill.

Locke, E. A., Latham, G. P., & Smith, K. J. (1990). *A theory of goal setting & task performance.* Englewood Cliffs, N.J.: Prentice-Hall.

Locke, E. A., Shaw, K. N., Saari, L. M., & Latham, G. P. (1981). Goal setting and task performance. *Psychological Bulletin*, 90(1), 125-152.

Seijts, G. H., & Latham, G. P. (2001). The effect of distal learning, outcome, and proximal goals on a moderately complex task. *Journal of Organizational Behavior*, 22(3), 291-307.

Smith, K. G., Locke, E. A., & Barry, D. (1990). Goal setting, planning, and organizational performance: An experimental simulation. *Organizational Behavior and Human Decision Processes*, 46(1), 118-134.

Weldon, E., & Weingart, L. R. (1993). Group goals and group performance. *British Journal of Social Psychology*, 32(4), 307-334.

Wood, R. E., & Locke, E. A. (1990). Goal setting and strategy effects on complex tasks. In B. Staw & L. L. Cummings (Eds.), *Research in organizational behavior*, Vol. 12 (pp. 73-109).

MOTIVATION

Cameron, J., & Pierce, W. D. (1996). The debate about rewards and intrinsic motivation: Protests and accusations do not alter the results. *Review of Educational Research*, 66(1), 39.

Deci, E. L. (1971). Effects of externally mediated rewards on intrinsic motivation. *Journal of Personality and Social Psychology*, 18(1), 105-115.

Deci, E. L. (1975). *Intrinsic motivation.* New York: Plenum Press.

Deci, E. L., Koestner, R., & Ryan, R. M. (1999). A meta-analytic review of experiments examining the effects of extrinsic rewards on intrinsic motivation. *Psychological Bulletin*, 125(6), 627-668.

Deci, E. L., Koestner, R., & Ryan, R. M. (2001). Extrinsic rewards and intrinsic motivation in education: Reconsidered once again.

Review of Educational Research, 71(1), 1-27.

Deci, E. L., & Ryan, R. M. (1985). *Intrinsic motivation and self-determination in human behavior.* New York: Plenum Press.

Deci, E. L., & Ryan, R. M. (1991). *A motivational approach to self: Integration in personality.* Proceedings from Nebraska Symposium on Motivation 1990, Lincoln, NE.

Eisenberger, R., & Cameron, J. (1996). Detrimental effects of reward: Reality or myth? *American Psychologist*, 51(11), 1153-1166.

Hackman, J. R., & Oldham, G. R. (1976). Motivation through the design of work. *Organizational Behavior and Human Performance*, 16, 250-279.

Herzberg, F. (1966). *Work and the nature of man.* Cleveland, OH: The World Publishing Company.

Herzberg, F. (1968). One more time: How do you motivate employees? *Harvard Business Review*, 46(1), 53-62.

Herzberg, F. (1973). *Work and the nature of man.* New York: New American Library.

Herzberg, F., Mausner, B., Peterson, R. O., & Capwell, D. F. (1957). *Job attitudes: Review of research and opinion.* Pittsburgh, PA: Psychological Service of Pittsburgh.

Herzberg, F., Mausner, B., & Snyderman, B. B. (1959). *The motivation to work* (2nd ed.). New York: Wiley.

McGregor, D. M. (1957). The human side of enterprise. *Management Review*, 46, 22-28, 88-92.

McGregor, D. M. (1960). *The human side of enterprise.* New York: McGraw-Hill.

Ryan, R. M., & Deci, E. L. (2000). Self-determination theory and the facilitation of intrinsic motivation, social development, and well-being. *American Psychologist*, 55(1), 68-78.

Vroom, V. H. (1964). *Work and motivation*. Oxford, England: Wiley.

TEAM MODELS

Bales, R. F. (1953). The equilibrium process in small groups. In T. Parson, R. F. Bales, & E. A. Shils (Eds.), *Working Papers in the Theory of Action* (pp. 111-161). Glencoe, IL: Free Press.

Bales, R. F., & Strodtbeck, F. L. (1951). Phases in group problem-solving. *Journal of Abnormal Social Psychology*, 46(4), 485-495.

Bales, R. F., & Strodtbeck, F. L. (1968). Phases in group problem-solving. In D. Cartwright & A. Zander (Eds.), *Group dynamics: Research and theory* (3rd ed., pp. 389-398). New York: Harper & Row.

Gersick, C. J. G. (1988). Time and transition in work teams: Toward a new model of group development. *Academy of Management Journal*, 31(1), 9-41.

Gersick, C. J. G. (1989). Marking time: Predictable transitions in task groups. *Academy of Management Journal*, 32(2), 274-309.

McGrath, J. E. (1964). *Social psychology: A brief introduction*. New York: Holt, Rinehart and Winston.

McGrath, J. E. (1991). Time, interaction, and performance (TIP): A theory of groups. *Small Group Research*, 22(2), 147-174.

Tuckman, B. W. (1965). Developmental sequence in small groups. *Psychological Bulletin*, 63(6), 384-399.

Tuckman, B. W., & Jensen, M. A. C. (1977). Stages of small-group development revisited. *Group & Organization Management*, 2(4), 419-427.

MINDFULNESS

Baer, R. A., Smith, G. T., Lykins, E., Button, D., Krietemeyer, J., Sauer, S. et al. (2008). Construct validity of the five facet mindfulness questionnaire in meditating and nonmeditating samples. *Assessment, 15*(3), 329-342.

INDEX